"Tell me, Molly. Tell me what you're feeling."

She shivered. "Much, ~~the time time. It's too~~ much." She pushed him slightly away from her. "I didn't think…" Her words trailed off and she dropped her head to his shoulder. "I *can't* think."

Sam understood. He'd had weeks to consider his attraction to Molly, what he wanted and how he wanted to pursue her. Unless he missed his guess, she hadn't even realized what she was feeling until earlier today. He wrapped both arms around her and pulled her close so she could feel the warmth and hardness of his body.

Molly shivered again and leaned against him. Her lips met his, kissing and probing, tasting and experimenting.

"It's okay," he assured her. "I'm not trying to rush you into anything. I just want you to know how much I *want* you."

"Whatever I'm feeling," she whispered, "it's not rushed."

# WANT AD WEDDING
## Neesa Hart

# HARLEQUIN®

TORONTO • NEW YORK • LONDON
AMSTERDAM • PARIS • SYDNEY • HAMBURG
STOCKHOLM • ATHENS • TOKYO • MILAN • MADRID
PRAGUE • WARSAW • BUDAPEST • AUCKLAND

ISBN 0-373-75008-0

WANT AD WEDDING

This edition published by arrangement with Harlequin Books S.A.

® and TM are trademarks of the publisher. Trademarks indicated with ® are registered in the United States Patent and Trademark Office, the Canadian Trade Marks Office and in other countries.

Visit us at www.eHarlequin.com

**Printed in U.S.A.**

## ABOUT THE AUTHOR

Neesa Hart is the multipublished, award-winning author of more than twenty books. Her other titles for Harlequin American Romance include *Who Gets To Marry Max* and *Her Passionate Pirate*. She lives in central Virginia, where she is hard at work writing her next novel and her second children's choir musical. You can reach Neesa at neesa@infoline.net.

Dear Reader,

People are always asking writers, "Where do you get your ideas?" and to be perfectly honest, I don't always have an answer. Usually the *real* answer is something like, "Oh, well, I was at the beauty shop reading a magazine when I saw an article that reminded me of a person I knew in high school who now works for a major corporation and I remembered that she had the same color hair as the woman in the picture, which made me wonder if that particular color would look good as paint on someone's wall, and if so, what kind of decorator would apply it and how would her client react?" Um, yeah.

But in the case of *Want Ad Wedding*, I actually have an answer I can share with you! I have a very good friend who got me hooked on the intrigue and pleasure of reading personal ads. The tiny little biographies are fascinating. I was reading the ads in our local paper one day and saw an odd one that essentially said, "I hope I never see you again," which naturally made me wonder what had inspired a person to pay money to print something like that. Was it a rash act, like an e-mail fired off without forethought? Did the advertiser now regret putting the words in print? And if he or she did, could the situation be salvaged?

So *Want Ad Wedding* was born. And what kind of hero could I pair with a headstrong, impulsive, act-without-thinking heroine? A master of self-control and decorum, of course—just to keep things interesting. Throw in some hometown fun, a few ducks and a host of eccentric family members and *Bam!* Fireworks.

Enjoy!

*Neesa Hart*

## Chapter One

WANTED: self-assured, confident woman to mend ways of arrogant confirmed bachelor. Sam Reed, Operating Partner and CFO of Reed Enterprises, seeks a candidate of marriageable age who is looking for a serious commitment. The ideal woman must be able to tolerate arbitrary decisions, poor communication skills, lack of responsiveness, ice-cold glares, periodic tantrums and smugness. Mr. Reed also possesses a vengeful nature that makes indefatigable patience a necessity. Candidates must be willing to accept years of frustration and irritation in exchange for sharing Reed family fortune and domiciles. Due to Mr. Reed's lengthy business trips and frequent travel, benefits of this position include long periods of solitude, separation, and downtime. Interested candidates may apply directly to Mr. Reed, c/o the *Payne Sentinel,* Payne Massachusetts.

Aunt Ida always said, ''Wear your best on your worst day. Because days come and go—but looking good is what counts.''

Molly Flynn always made a point of taking her aunt Ida's advice. So on Monday morning, she'd ironed her best pair of jeans, pulled on a new University of Delaware sweatshirt, and put new laces in her sneakers before heading off to work. Today, she figured, was quite possibly going to be the worst day of her life. After berating herself for the carelessness, impulsivity and outright idiocy that had gotten her into this mess, she'd managed to pull herself together after a stern lecture to her reflection in the mirror. As Aunt Ida always said, Flynns were not quitters. Flynns did not hide from their mistakes. Flynns had pluck.

Actually, Aunt Ida had referred to Flynn tenacity as an unmentionable part of the male anatomy. But ever since her mother had washed Molly's mouth out with soap for repeating the phrase at dinner one night, Molly had called it *pluck*.

But that morning, she'd given her reflection a knowing look that said she meant exactly what Aunt Ida had said.

Then she'd splashed enough cold water on her face to diminish the bluish circles under eyes, whipped through her usual ten-minute routine of light makeup and strong coffee; wrestled with her lamentably curly red hair until it became apparent that even her hair was going to get the better of her today; and made her way to the *Payne Sentinel* offices in historic downtown Payne, Massachusetts, where she was going to get fired as soon as Sam Reed got to the office.

She'd felt vaguely like a condemned prisoner making her way to the guillotine. Her fate was inevitable.

The only thing she could control was how she reacted to it.

And Flynns never cowered.

So Molly leaned back in her battered chair in the *Payne Sentinel* copy office and stole a glance at the clock. 8:58. Two minutes and counting.

"All right, Molly—" Cindy Freesdon entered the copy office, dropped her purse to the floor and pulled a chair up to the edge of Molly's desk. She pinned her with an avidly curious look. "Give, babe. When were you planning to tell us you and Reed were, you know, *friendly?*"

Molly stifled a groan. Humiliation was bad enough, but *public* humiliation was far worse. She wished Sam Reed would hurry up and drag his predictable, irascible, temperamental, bullheaded self to work and be done with this so she could clean out her desk and go home.

She gritted her teeth and met the probing look in Cindy's blue eyes. "It's not like that," she assured her friend. "You don't understand."

Cindy dangled the Personals section between her thumb and forefinger. "I read the morning edition while I was getting dressed." She indicated the copy room where the activity level had already reached light speed. "You're the one who placed this ad for Reed. It's got your sense of humor all over it."

Molly forced herself not to flinch. "Not on purpose."

That sent Cindy's eyebrows into her bleached blond bangs. "Oh, this is too wicked."

"Do you think everyone else knows?"

"My phone started ringing ten minutes after the paper landed on my doorstep. I tried to squelch the gossip, but even I don't have that much power."

That won a halfhearted laugh from Molly. Cindy Freesdon was the *Sentinel*'s resident busybody. She didn't doubt that all interested parties would have turned to Cindy for information when the inflammatory personal ad showed up in the *Sentinel*'s Monday edition. "Thanks," she told Cindy. "I'm already going to get fired. I'd rather not be humiliated on top of it."

Cindy pursed her lips. "I hate to break it to you, but it's kind of a lost cause. If it makes you feel any better, I did make them feel guilty as sin about it." She shrugged slightly. "There's not a person in this room you haven't bailed out at one time or another."

"This is my family," Molly said simply. "I've always thought of it that way."

"That's obvious." Cindy tapped a long fingernail on Molly's overladen desk. "So that's why everyone's pretty much drawn the same conclusion— there's no way you would have risked what you've got here by running that ad simply because you were miffed about the argument you and Reed had on Friday."

"You don't think so?"

Cindy gave her a pointed look. "I may not be the investigative reporter you are, Molly, but I know a lover's tiff when I see one."

Molly exhaled a weary breath. "I don't suppose it would do me any good to deny that."

"Probably not."

"It's a long story. It was a joke—my friend, Jo-

Anna—'' She shook her head. "I don't have time to explain it right now. He'll be here soon."

Cindy stole a glance at the clock. "Forty seconds, if he's on time."

"He's always on time."

"Good point." Cindy dropped the copy of the paper on Molly's desk. "Lunch today? You can fill me in then."

"Sure. I'll be fired by then, anyway. At least I won't have to clock out," she said bitterly, the hated time clock—one of the many unwelcome changes Sam Reed had brought to the *Payne Sentinel.*

The antique clock that had kept vigil over the newsroom for nearly a century chimed nine. Precisely on schedule, the wide glass doors swung open, admitting a gust of chilly October air and forever suspending the rest of Cindy's comment. The usual busy hum of activity in the newsroom ground to a halt. Fingers stopped typing, and chairs stopped creaking. Chatter ceased and pencils stilled. Only the lonely hum of a printer punctuated the eerie calm as one hundred eyes turned simultaneously to watch the drama unfolding at Molly's desk.

Pluck, Molly reminded herself, as she met the steel-colored gaze of Sam Reed. He had a right to be furious. Since she'd seen the morning paper, she'd known this was going to turn ugly. She'd seen Sam angry only once. A member of the editorial staff had deliberately fabricated a source—forcing the *Sentinel* to issue a public apology. The look Sam had given the man could have melted glass.

Molly fully expected to find that same look in his eyes when she met his gaze. What she found, instead, stole her breath. Yes, his normal cool, implacable calm was gone, but she couldn't quite pin a name to the expression in its place. A banked fire made his eyes look darker than usual—like storm-laden skies on a hot summer day. But what threw her the most was the slight sparkle that made him look as though he was enjoying himself.

This was going to be worse than she'd imagined, she thought with a sinking sense of dread.

Sam held her gaze for several long seconds, then announced a breezy "Good morning" to the staff. In the six weeks he had been running the paper, he'd arrived every morning at precisely nine o'clock. And every morning, he'd breezed through the newsroom without acknowledging the existence of the fifty or so employees who warily watched his daily trek to the elevator. No wonder then, Molly mused, that his butter-soft voice had the impact of a class-four tornado. She was surprised when the collective intake of breath didn't rustle the piles of papers on her desk.

Damn him, she thought as she studied his normally implacable features. Dark hair framed a face made of angles and planes. There wasn't a soft edge on the man. And he was definitely enjoying this. Like a cat, she mused, moving in on a helpless mouse and savoring the poor thing's moment of doom.

Sam crossed the two steps to her desk and subtly shifted his briefcase so Cindy had to ease to the side. He planted the Italian leather case amid the clutter and leaned in with the smooth confidence of a predator.

At least, Molly thought wryly, her colleagues would have something to remember when she was gone. The spectacle he was causing was the stuff newsroom lore was made of. Despite herself, she had to suppress a small bubble of amusement. She didn't think Sam would appreciate knowing that his legacy at the *Sentinel* was going to be reduced to newsroom gossip.

Something in her expression must have flickered, tipping him that he'd momentarily lost the upper hand. Swiftly, he produced a daisy from his left coat pocket with enough flourish to ensure he had her complete attention. He dropped it in her pencil cup, then leaned so close that Molly had to force herself not to retreat. While her colleagues raptly watched, Sam cupped Molly's face in his large hand and pressed his mouth to her ear. "In my office in ten minutes."

An unmistakable thread of steel undergirded the soft command. "Okay."

He stood, trailing his fingers along the line of her jaw as he stepped away from her desk. Flashing Cindy Freesdon his million-dollar smile, he brushed past her and made his way to the elevator.

The doors slid smoothly shut before anyone breathed. In the vacuum that followed, a small crowd formed around Molly's desk.

"My God, Molly." David Ward straightened his wire-frame glasses. "You really did run that ad, didn't you?"

Priscilla Lyons threw Cindy an accusing glance. "I told you." Priscilla pinned Molly with a hard look. "Come on, Molly—we're dying here. How long have you been involved with him?"

Molly reached for her patience. "This isn't what you think."

Priscilla's eyes twinkled. "No? Sparks have been flying between you two since he got here a few weeks ago."

David laughed. "A *daisy*, Molly?" He glanced at the pencil cup. "The man brought you a daisy."

Cindy laughed. "If it had been a rose, that might have been suspicious, but daisies? In October?"

"He's annoyed," Molly assured them.

"Mm-hmm." Priscilla looked unconvinced. "I wish someone would get annoyed with me that way." She rolled her eyes. "I can't believe I didn't see this coming."

That made Cindy chuckle. "It was the look in his eyes that practically did me in. Lord, did you feel the electricity popping in here?"

"My monitor dimmed," supplied one of the copy editors.

David planted his hands on Molly's desk. "We're your friends."

"We've been watching you and Reed go at each other for weeks," Priscilla added. "I should have known something was up."

"Nothing," Molly said through clenched teeth, "is going on."

Cindy tapped her fingernail on Molly's desk. "You can't leave us in suspense like this. It's not fair."

Molly stifled a weary sigh. As much as she enjoyed the family-type atmosphere at the *Sentinel,* today it was making her feel claustrophobic. She'd already ducked two calls from her sisters this morning before she'd left her apartment, and was certain the rest of

the Flynn clan would be calling for answers before
the day was out. Her family was nothing if not persistent. She reached for the envelope on the corner of
her desk, sliding it into her pocket as she stood up.
"Look. I have to get upstairs. He's expecting me."

"I'll bet," Priscilla drawled.

Molly ignored her. "I'll tell you all what happened
as soon as I get back."

"We'll be waiting," David assured her.


THREE MINUTES LATER, she walked into the outer office of the upstairs suite where Sam Reed controlled
the *Payne Sentinel*. Had it only been six weeks? It
felt like a lifetime. "Morning, Karen," she greeted
the young woman behind the reception desk. "He's
expecting me."

Karen gave her a sympathetic look. "So he said."
She shot a quick glance at his closed door, then
dropped her gaze to the classified section on her desk.
"Er, Molly—"

"It's a long story," Molly assured her.

"I can imagine."

Molly paused, deliberately stalling for time. "Do
you think he's going to kill me when I go in there?"

Karen's eyebrows knitted together in confusion.
"Nooooo," she said thoughtfully. "He didn't seem
mad or anything."

Molly didn't think that was a particularly good
sign. "No?"

"Uh-uh. He was, you know, like he usually is. Intense, only—" Karen seemed to search for a word.

"Darker?" Molly supplied.

Karen shook her head. "No, more like 'alive' or

something. Actually, I'd say he's in a pretty good mood." She glanced at the paper again. "Considering."

"Great."

Karen leaned closer. "Frankly, I thought the two of you were actually going to come to blows in that meeting on Friday."

"Me, too."

"So it really didn't surprise me—" The buzzer on her phone interrupted her. Karen gave a guilty start and punched the button. "Yes?"

"Is Miss Flynn here yet, Karen?"

"Yes, sir."

"Good." The soft click of his phone seemed to reverberate off the glass walls of the reception area.

Karen gave Molly a knowing look. "I guess you should go in."

Molly nodded, forcing a bright smile, and headed for the door to the lion's den. Sam pulled it open the instant she reached for the doorknob. Startled, she raised her gaze to his and saw a flinty look that quickly dissolved as he flashed an unusually warm smile. Was it her imagination, or was there a hint of steel in it? "Morning," he said quietly, then looked at Karen. "Hold my calls, will you, Karen?" He placed his hand at the small of Molly's back.

"Sure." Karen leaned back in her chair, her expression speculative.

Sam was already applying a subtle pressure to her back, leading her through the door. "This could take awhile."

The instant the door shut behind her, he dropped his hand, and walked to his desk in silence. When he had rounded it, he sat in the high leather chair and simply watched her with an enigmatic look in his eyes. Molly felt her sneakers sinking into the plush carpet. Like quicksand, she mused. She had to fight the urge to shuffle her feet. She'd seen a survival documentary once where the expert had explained that the surest way to die in quicksand was to fight the inevitable by thrashing around.

She pulled an envelope from her back pocket and headed for his desk. "Before you fire me," she said, "I can save you the trouble." She dropped the envelope. "That's my letter of resignation."

He said nothing. She tried not to squirm. This was beginning to feel like the time in kindergarten when she'd been called to the principal's office for slugging Carolyn Lockhardt on the playground. The man hadn't understood that Carolyn—with her perfect hair, perfect clothes and constant boasting about how she always colored inside the lines and moved her crayon in the same direction—had simply been begging for the punch. Every kindergarten kid had been on Molly's side. She'd become the hero of the bad colorers. The principal had given her a lecture on ladylike behavior and suspended her for two days.

Something told her that Sam Reed wouldn't let her off that easily. She forged ahead. "I—you don't have to accept it. You have the right to terminate me. You probably should terminate me." A voice inside her head was screaming at her to shut up, but his inscrutable expression wouldn't let her heed the voice. Once, just one time, she wanted to see him crack— even if it meant watching his temper explode. The day he'd fired Lawson Peters for faking a source, he'd been noticeably angry but completely controlled. Molly had watched the exchange, fascinated by the raw current of power that seemed to ripple just beneath the surface of Sam's facade. She had a feeling that if he ever released it, it would have the effect of a volcano. ''It was a stupid thing to do,'' she continued. ''And for what it's worth, I never intended it to actually run in the paper. I was angry at you on Friday.''

She paused, hoping he'd at least acknowledge her with a tilt of his head or a slight compression of his firm mouth. Anything. He sat statue-still. Molly waded out a little deeper. ''When you wouldn't listen to me about the transportation hub story, I lost my temper.'' An understatement, she knew. She'd lost her cool in the editorial meeting when he'd refused to explore the validity of the story in favor of a community action piece he'd assigned to another writer. The depth of her reaction had surprised Molly herself, but not when she weighed it against the pressure of dealing with his heavy-handed management for the past six weeks. By Friday afternoon, she'd had all she could take. She'd exploded in a fit of temper that had left no doubt about the extent of her frustration. Sam had waited out her tirade in silence, then infuriated her by simply ignoring the outburst and continuing with his elaboration on the article he'd assigned.

Furious, Molly had left the meeting with a pounding headache and a hammering pulse. She couldn't decide whether she was angrier with him for his condescending attitude, or with herself for letting him get to her.

Molly shook her head and shoved her hands into

the back pockets of her jeans. Sam still said nothing. He wasn't going to make this easy for her. He had no reason to, she thought grimly. She'd brought this on herself. "Regardless," she said wearily, "running the ad was irresponsible and unprofessional. I'm sure it made you uncomfortable, and if you want to fire me for it, then I understand. I can have my desk cleaned out by the end of the day."

An uncomfortable silence began to spin its web in the stillness of his office. Molly fought the urge to fill the void. Finally, when her nerves were practically screaming for relief, he blinked. "Finished?" he asked softly.

She nodded. "Um, yes."

"Good. Sit down."

She didn't have the energy to decide whether or not the proprietary command annoyed her. She dropped gratefully into the leather chair. He reached for his briefcase. The sound of the locks snapping open seemed unnaturally loud in the stillness of his office. Sam pulled the classified section from the briefcase and flipped it onto his desk.

Molly closed her eyes and waited for humiliation.

"I had no idea you were quite this—eloquent."

He couldn't possibly be teasing her. Could he? Her eyes popped open. "I minored in creative writing in college."

"It shows." He glanced at the newspaper. "Arbitrary decisions," he read. He captured her gaze. "They aren't arbitrary."

Dear God. He *was* teasing her. "Er—"

"Periodic tantrums?" he continued, looking at the ad once more. "Smugness? I am never smug."

The audacity of the statement made her mouth drop. "You have got to be kidding."

She had been prepared for a blistering lecture and a dismissal. The hint of humor in his tone had her so off-guard that she found herself uncharacteristically speechless. Sam pushed the paper aside and regarded her with his frank, disarming stare. "What the hell *were* you thinking, Molly?"

The question was soft, and strangely curious. There was no demand in it. That had to be the reason why the explanation came so readily to her lips. "I—it's silly," she admitted. "Actually, it's worse than silly. It's humiliating and stupid." She paused while her sense of justice convinced her pride that she owed Sam this explanation. "It was just a diversion that my friend JoAnna and I used in college—to de-stress and vent our frustrations. The two of us ran the university paper. One end-of-the-week challenge was to fill all the little spaces where the stories ran short."

"Stringing," he stated.

"Sort of. Stringers use *actual* material. We just made up ads. You know—stuff like, 'for the secrets of the ancients, send one dollar to the following P.O. Box.'"

Sam nodded. "Most college papers have those."

"And when people particularly annoyed us, we wrote ads about them."

"Personal ads," he guessed.

"Yes. It helped blow off steam." She frowned as she recalled her mood from Friday afternoon. "After the editorial meeting—I was so angry at you."

"You thought I shot down your article concept."

"You did—"

"I didn't. I just wasn't finished with the piece we were already discussing. You have a habit of not letting me finish."

Molly's head started to ache. The conversation seemed almost surreal. For six weeks, she had wanted to strangle this man. He'd walked into the *Payne Sentinel* and taken over with the high-handedness of an Eastern potentate. While everyone knew the *Sentinel* was struggling financially, no one had suspected the extent of the trouble until Carl Morgan, the *Sentinel*'s owner, brought in Sam Reed to bail them out. He was part of Reed Enterprises' vast publishing machine, and he had a reputation for taking small-market publications and folding them into large distribution conglomerates.

Unpredictable by reputation, Sam was the illegitimate son of publishing legend Edward Reed. Before his death, the old man had controlled a staggering fifteen percent of the daily periodicals in the United States. Sam had entered the Reed empire at age nine when, in a spectacularly publicized incident, his mother had announced to a press hungry for Edward Reed's humiliation, that Sam was his child. Her emotional statement had laid out details of a month-long affair. She'd never told Edward of the child, she'd claimed, because she feared his retribution. Economic hardship and a guilty conscience had finally driven her to reveal the truth.

With his notorious élan, Edward had called her bluff. He'd acknowledged Sam as his son and taken him to live in the Reed household. The press, deprived of a longed-for spectacle, had quickly lost interest. Sam, and Edward's legitimate son, Ben Reed, had inherited Reed Publishing when Edward died fifteen years later. Together, the two men had built the company from a feared bully into an admired success. Ben Reed, sources said, was the methodical one on the team. He did the planning while his brother was the maverick who took the risks and turned would-be failures into success stories.

And Molly didn't like his vision for the *Sentinel*.

They'd clashed immediately. He was slowly doing away with the paper's more serious content and expanding its community focus. Soon, she feared, the *Sentinel* would be nothing more than a coupon clipper.

She'd worked at the *Sentinel* since she'd been old enough for her first paper route. Nobody knew the paper, or its subscribers, she figured, as well as she did. But Sam had turned down every suggestion she'd made. He'd locked himself away in this office, making it clear to the staff that they could do his bidding or quit. Editorial meetings had turned into sparring matches, where Molly stood up to him and he shot her down.

In the six weeks since Carl had introduced him as the man who was going to save the *Sentinel,* Molly had yet to see him show a human side. Until now. When he should be furious. When she'd finally given him the right to be furious. She couldn't wait to find out what her sisters would say about this.

''Mr. Reed—'' she began.

He held up a hand. It wasn't the manicured, soft-looking hand of an idle businessman, she noted with some fascination. He had calluses on his palm, and new-looking scrapes that skimmed the edge of his blunt fingers. How was it that she'd never noticed his hands before? "Like now," he said. "I'm not finished telling you why I cut you off about that story."

Molly frowned. He shook his head. She swore the sparkle was back in his eyes, turning the steel color a softer shade of gray. "I bug the hell out of you," he said, "don't I?"

"Yes."

The flat response made him laugh. The rich laugh surprised her. It came easily and sounded well-used. Where, she wondered, was the Sam Reed she'd been sparring with in editorial meetings? He steepled his hands beneath his chin and gave her a dry look. "So you made me the victim of a personal ad to your friend?"

Molly nodded. "JoAnna called on Friday afternoon. She usually does. It's a ritual we've had since we graduated." If a person could die from embarrassment, Molly figured, she would become an obituary at any moment. In hindsight, it all seemed extremely juvenile. Even trying to explain it only seemed to make it worse, but her sense of honor demanded that she take the licks. "I was angry. I vented. JoAnna was having a lousy day, too. She reminded me of the game. I wrote the ad and e-mailed it to her. I thought it would make her laugh. I forgot to clear it from my screen before I left for the night."

"And the stringer found it and diligently put it into copy by the Saturday-morning deadline for today's personals," he guessed.

"Yes." Molly rubbed her palms on the rough fabric of her jeans. "I didn't know until this morning."

"Imagine *my* surprise."

There it was again, that slight thread of humor in his tone. Molly grimaced. "I was mortified. I'm sure it was worse for you. I—it was childish and irresponsible. There's nothing I could say that would adequately apologize."

He picked up the unopened envelope that held her resignation. "So you came in prepared to quit?"

"It seemed like the most honorable thing to do."

He nodded, his expression thoughtful. With a quick twist of his wrist, he tore the envelope in two and tossed it into his trash can. "Think of something else."

Molly stared at him. "I beg your pardon?"

"Think of something else. You're the best journalist this paper has. You should probably be working in a bigger market—"

"I don't want to work in a bigger market."

"Let me *finish,* Molly," he said, and damned if his lips didn't twitch into a half smile. "You should probably be working in a larger market, but you decided to stay here. Why?"

"It's my home." She shrugged. "My family lives here. I've worked for the *Sentinel* since I was eleven years old."

"Paper route?"

"Yes."

He nodded. "First job?"

"If you don't count weeding Mrs. Ellerby's vegetable garden."

"That was seasonal work. It's different."

Molly had no response to that, so she simply watched him. The collar of his white shirt lay in stark contrast to the bronzed column of his throat. Was it her imagination, or was his tan deeper this morning than it had been on Friday? She simply couldn't picture him doing anything as mundane or sedentary as strolling along the beach at Martha's Vineyard. She thought about the scrape she'd seen on his fingers and could easily imagine him, shirtless, laboring under the afternoon sun. Maybe on a sailboat, though even that seemed too much like recreation. He leaned back in his chair and placed his hands behind his head. ''My first job was a paper route. I liked the way the papers smelled when I picked them up.''

The admission surprised her, and yet, it didn't. Edward Reed's son probably wouldn't have needed a paper route for spending money. The renowned media mogul could well afford to give his son a generous allowance. Though few people in the industry were unaware that Sam was Reed's illegitimate son, Reed had made his acceptance of the child abundantly clear. But, the same thing that told her he didn't spend weekends at the beach said he hadn't spent his childhood living on his father's money. ''Did you have to roll and band them for delivery when you picked them up, or did they come that way?''

''I did it,'' he said with a slight nod. ''Kids today have it easy. They get those plastic bags.''

''Rolling's half the skill,'' she concurred. ''If you don't tuck the edges, you can't toss the paper right.''

''Comes unwrapped in midair.''

''Plus you get paper cuts when you pull 'em from the bag.''

He smiled. It was dazzling. Molly couldn't ever recall seeing him smile so naturally. This was a smile straight from a remembered pleasure. Her heart skipped a beat. His eyes crinkled at the corners when he smiled. The observation surprised her. The slight lines suggested that his smile, like his laugh, was something he used often. "The day I finally mastered the doormat toss onto old man Greely's porch—" he shrugged "—I felt like Nolan Ryan pitching a no hitter." The faraway look left his eyes as he met her gaze again. "He had shrubs. Boxwoods. They blocked the sidewalk."

Molly nodded. "I had a house like that. You had to float the paper over the shrubs so it landed on the mat."

"Um. And Greely had a covered porch. So the paper had to go between the roof of the porch and the boxwoods and land on the mat—"

They said in unison, "Without hitting the door."

Molly laughed. "I'm impressed. I was pretty good, but not that good."

"I practiced for weeks."

"I hope he tipped well."

"I don't think I ever got a tip out of the man. But he didn't yell at me for hitting his door either. And when the paper I worked for threatened to take away my route and consolidate it into truck delivery, he went to the circulation director and saved my job. I never knew what he told that guy, but I kept the route until I graduated from high school." He shook his head. "The day I graduated, Fred Greely sent me a check for a hundred dollars."

Molly found her first smile of the morning. "No wonder you love the newspaper business."

"Just like you?" he asked softly.

She hesitated. "Yes. Just like me."

"I thought so. So find something else. You can't quit."

"I'm not sure what you mean," she said carefully.

Sam pushed the paper aside and folded his hands on his desk. "May I make a suggestion?"

"Since when do you *ask* me if you can make a suggestion?" she quipped.

Another slight smile. The dent—dare she call it a dimple—in his left cheek deepened when he smiled. And that dimple, that infuriatingly devilish dimple, did something to his face that made her stop breathing.

Oh, dear Lord, she thought, as she felt the flutter in the pit of her stomach, and recognized the way her lungs constricted. It can't be. It can't and must not be. But even as she struggled for breath and pressed a hand to her belly, she knew the signs. They were horrifying and impossible evidence that she found the man attractive. Her sisters had been telling her for weeks that the animosity she felt toward him was one step away from passion. She'd denied it. Vehemently. Too vehemently. With the sun glinting on his dark hair, and his damned dimple making her body temperature notch up, she had to fight the urge to bury her face in her hands.

Not again, she told herself fiercely. And for God's sake not now. For years, she'd known that she had a chronic habit of falling for unsuitable men. With the same reckless abandon she lived life, she'd tumbled headfirst into relationships. Her sisters had been warning her for years. If they found out she'd fallen for Sam Reed, she'd never hear the end of it. Blissfully, Sam seemed unaware of her momentary lapse into insanity. He chuckled softly at her quip, and the sound made her stomach flip-flop. "Oh, no," Molly muttered beneath her breath.

"What?"

"Nothing," she assured him, fiercely demanding that her nerves quiet down. "You were saying?" she asked with a feeling of dread.

He looked at her curiously but continued, "I was saying that I'd like to offer you a way to make reparations for this—indiscretion."

"What do you want?" she asked warily. She had a sinking feeling that whatever it was, it would be far worse than losing her job.

"I want you to have dinner with me."

## Chapter Two

She was sputtering. There wasn't any other way to describe it, he thought, fascinated. Sam Reed was fairly certain he'd never seen a woman sputter. He watched her closely as she struggled for breath. "Dinner? With you? You mean, like a date?"

He was screwing this up, he thought wearily. No big surprise there. How he managed to succeed in business and fail so spectacularly at anything requiring tact, he hadn't a clue. He'd obviously inherited the trait from his father. "Like a date," he affirmed carefully, wondering why the word seemed so old-fashioned and quaint. He frequently took women to social events. He'd had his share of lovers. But he hadn't "dated" since high school. "Don't you have them?" She drew her eyebrows together in a sharp frown. Was baffled or just annoyed.

"Excuse me?"

He didn't think he was imagining the way the spray of freckles on her nose had blended with the heightening color in her face. From the day he'd met her, he'd found Molly Flynn's freckles fascinating. They formed a steady trail, which disappeared beneath the collar of her sweatshirt. The thought of following that line of freckles to its end made his mouth water—that and her maple-leaf–red hair and her eyes the color of summer clover. Nothing about Molly Flynn was bland. She had vibrancy and life—something Sam had begun to fear he himself was missing.

Perhaps that explained why he'd caught himself imagining her lingerie. Sam had never found speculating on women's lingerie to be particularly time worthy, but this was different. He had an unshakeable feeling that underneath her ubiquitous jeans and sweatshirts were laces and satins in a range of colors and styles that would knock his socks off.

He forced himself to concentrate on getting her to agree to a date. Plenty of time later to contemplate her lingerie. He wasn't used to explaining himself, and he didn't do it well. If the look of absolute confusion on her face was any indication, he was definitely screwing this up. "Maybe I should elaborate," he suggested, more for his own benefit than hers.

"Maybe." She fidgeted a little in the chair. He noted that about her, too. She never sat still. He, on the other hand, could sit absolutely still for hours. But Molly was perpetual motion. It should have annoyed him. He still hadn't figured out why it didn't. The only thing he knew for sure was that he wanted her. He'd started wanting her when she'd challenged him in their first editorial meeting. He had kept on wanting her right through their near shouting match on Friday afternoon. When he'd awakened to his sister's phone call about the personal ad in the morning's *Payne Sentinel*, his mind had immediately recognized the opportunity. If Molly would only cooperate.

''When Carl hired me to put the *Sentinel* back in the black, I almost turned him down. Reed Enterprises is negotiating several other ventures right now, and my brother, Ben, had asked me to manage a project in London.''

Molly nodded. ''Reed Enterprises is working a merger with the *Daily*. I read about it in the trades.''

One of the sexiest things about Molly Flynn, he thought with satisfaction, was her brain. Sam had always preferred sharp-witted lovers, and Molly's brain was razor-sharp. ''But Carl's an old friend. He helped me through college. I owe him.''

''He respects you. He trusts you.''

''He loves this paper,'' Sam assured her. ''And he loves the people who work here.''

Molly studied him for a moment. ''You're trying to change it. Carl never wanted the *Sentinel* to become a community newsletter. He always wanted a serious journalistic paper geared for a small-town readership.''

''And he can have that. But without a few changes, the *Sentinel* can't turn a profit. The market has changed. Carl hasn't changed with it.''

''I still think the transportation hub piece is a good idea,'' she said. ''It's relevant. It's local. And it's got bite.''

''Would it surprise you to learn that I think it's a good idea, too?''

She frowned. ''But you said—''

He shook his head with a slight laugh. ''Because you didn't let me finish.'' At her sharp glare, he suppressed a grin. He was seriously pissing her off, he suspected, but she was still too embarrassed to storm out on him. At least he had that in his favor. "We're going to have to work on that."

"Before or after dinner?" she asked dryly.

"Before." He had other plans for after. Sam leaned back in his chair and felt himself relax. She was still listening. That had to be a good sign. "Here's the thing," he began. In business and in life, he'd always found it best to lay these matters out in a methodical fashion. Some women couldn't handle that, but Molly was brilliant and capable. Though she had a reckless streak that made her act impulsively, he was fairly certain she'd respond to logic. "This ad—it has raised questions in my family."

"I'll bet."

Her expression told him nothing. He sensed Molly was deeply embarrassed, but she was masking it well, facing the consequences with a courage he admired. "My brother, Ben, got married last year. His wife is—unconventional."

He detected a slight smile at the corners of her mouth. "So I've heard."

He didn't doubt it. His brother's engagement and marriage had been widely publicized. Sam shrugged. "I like Amy. A lot, actually. And now that my family knows her, they adore her as well. But the relationship has been a little tumultuous."

"And now that your brother has tied the knot, everyone is looking for a new target."

He thought of his aunt's phone call that morning and grimaced. She was the latest to join the campaign with his stepmother and half sister. "You could say that."

"And you're it."

He nodded. "Both my stepmother and sister have been scheming for years to get me down the aisle. My sister's hobby is planning weddings—hers, and other people's. Now she's got my aunt and my sister-in-law involved. At least Ben is smart enough to leave me alone, but the women are making me feel like George Custer at the Battle of Little Big Horn."

Molly chuckled, and it heightened the gold flecks in her green eyes. Sam had always liked Molly's eyes. They were expressive and revealing. He saw passion and intelligence in them—a combination he found irresistibly sexy. "I know the feeling," she assured him. "I've got four older sisters."

"My last relationship came to a spectacular end." Though her gaze had turned curious, he forged ahead. Time enough to explain Pamela later. "I was actually looking forward to going to London for Ben."

"And then the *Payne Sentinel* got in your way."

"Hmm," he concurred. "And in case you haven't noticed, I'm having difficulty getting people here to trust me."

"I think it's your car," she said, her tone serious.

"My car?"

"You drive a sports car. The only people in Payne who drive sports cars are insurance salesmen and morticians. You figure it out."

He stifled a laugh. He couldn't remember the last time a woman beyond his immediate family had made him feel like laughing. "Minivans and SUVs?"

"Or four-door sedans. Payne is that kind of place."

"You drive a '72 Beetle." It was sunset orange and had a hell of an exhaust problem. He'd have to convince her to let him take a look at that.

"I'm the town rebel." She drummed her fingers on the arm of the chair. "There's only room for one, you know."

"If I can get the staff of the *Sentinel* to follow my lead, I can save this paper," he said more seriously. "But frankly, you've got everyone thinking they have to choose sides between you and me. Right now, they're walking the fence because they're afraid for their jobs." He shook his head. "But if you force them to choose, they'll follow you." He leveled a hard look at her. "Even if it's right off a cliff. If you want the *Sentinel* to survive, you will have to accept some changes."

"Just because I don't agree with every decision you make doesn't mean I'm not willing to accept change."

"Then prove it to me." He leaned forward and planted his hands on the desk. "Convince me."

"Meaning *date* you?"

What, Sam wondered, slightly annoyed, was so damned unbelievable about the concept of having dinner with him. He had it on relatively good authority that he was considered highly eligible.

Ben would've reminded him that wooing women was nothing like negotiating contracts. It was five times harder, took ten times longer, and required twenty times the effort. Sam carefully chose his next words. "I'm talking about a business arrangement," he said softly. "A contract. Everyone in this town trusts you. If they perceive that you trust me, they will as well. This ad—" He thumped the paper with his knuckles. "People are asking questions. I want to give them answers that satisfy their curiosity without appearing to look like I have lost control.''

''But I didn't mean—''

He headed off her argument. He'd learned in the last six weeks that letting Molly reach full steam was never a good idea. ''And the people in Payne aren't the only issue. You can imagine how my sister reacted. The fact that a woman finally got the best of me has her positively ecstatic.''

Molly winced. ''Sorry.''

''And it's going to be embarrassing if I have to explain this by saying that you blew up at me at a meeting.'' He looked at her narrowly. ''I would think you'd find it pretty humiliating yourself.''

''I do,'' she insisted.

''But if people believe we are romantically involved, they'll brush this off as a lover's quarrel. We'll take a couple of jabs about it. Then the whole thing'll just blow over. You'll be lauded for having gotten the better of me. And if my family believes that I've finally found a woman who will put up with me, they'll—'' He stopped. He wasn't ready to elaborate yet. It was more information than he wanted Molly to have. ''There will be no embarrassing explanations nor apologies.''

''No one is going to believe that you and I are romantically involved. Not after what they've seen for the last six weeks.''

He shrugged. ''People see what they want to see. A few public appearances, a couple of social engagements, and everyone will be saying they knew it all along.''

"So you want me to pretend I'm involved with you?"

"No," he said carefully. "There's no pretense about it. I don't play games."

She frowned at him. "You've lost me."

Sam took a deep breath. The crucial part of any negotiation was where both parties tipped their hands. He was about to show Molly his cards, and he was gambling she'd do the same. "I don't want you to pretend to be involved, Molly," he said quietly. "I want you to *get* involved."

Her eyes widened. She stared at him for a full fifteen seconds. Sam was fairly certain he heard his watch ticking. He'd negotiated billion-dollar deals where he'd been far less tense. Somewhere in the back of his mind was the thought that it shouldn't be so damned hard to ask the woman for a date. But then, he'd never known a woman quite like Molly. Her lips pursed slightly as she stared at him. Finally, she muttered, "Oh."

Not the most enthusiastic response he'd ever received, but manageable. She hadn't said no. That's what counted. "I'll get to know you," he explained slowly. "You'll get to know me. And I'd like exclusive rights to your social life for a while. In exchange, I'll give you exclusive rights to mine." He was vaguely aware of how stuffy he sounded. *Smooth, Reed.* Why didn't he just go ahead and hand her a contract to sign.

"That's got to be the most romantic offer I've ever had," Molly quipped.

At least she hadn't stormed out. He considered that a good sign. Just as he'd thought, Molly Flynn was different from other women he'd known. "What have you got to lose?" he prompted.

She was drumming her fingers on her leg again, a quick, agitated rhythm that mirrored the pace of the thoughts he saw moving across her expressive face. "How long is this arrangement going to last?"

Sam realized that he'd been holding his breath when her question tipped him that she was seriously considering his offer. Years of business negotiations told him he was a few well-chosen words from closing the deal. "As long as we can stand each other," he assured her.

She hitched up the corners of her mouth. "We won't make it out the door on the first night."

He could only hope that the energy between them could be harnessed into something more satisfying than animosity. He'd felt considerably better when he'd finally admitted to himself that he was attracted to her. It explained why she got under his skin. "Actually, I have it on excellent authority that I can be very charming."

"I'd like to see that."

He leaned closer. "Then how about right now?"

"Right now?"

He nodded. "I've got a meeting with the mayor and the head of the transportation commission in thirty minutes. I thought you might like to go with me."

He could practically see the wheels turning in her head. After arguing with him for weeks about the importance of the *Sentinel*'s covering the Payne Board of Supervisors' approval of a major transportation hub development contract, she'd be unable to resist the opportunity to sit in on the meeting with two of the key players. ''Won't the mayor think it's odd if I tag along?''

Sam shrugged. ''You're our top reporter. Why should he think it's odd?''

She studied him warily. ''Because he has no reason to suspect you're planning an in-depth story about the hub.''

''Of course he has,'' Sam stated flatly. ''It's the biggest piece of local news on the horizon.''

''You've been telling me for weeks you didn't think it was newsworthy.''

''I didn't think the time was right,'' he told her flatly. ''I thought I had made that clear.''

Molly's eyebrows rose. ''I don't think anyone else in Friday's meeting got that impression.''

''Sorry to hear that. I have every intention of covering this story, and I have every intention of putting you on it.'' She was watching him with keen interest, he noted, as if she weren't quite sure she could trust him. He'd obviously misstepped there, if he'd made her doubt his intentions.

''You're serious,'' Molly said slowly. ''Aren't you?''

Sam nodded. ''Completely. I think the time is now right, and I'd planned to ask you to this meeting anyway. The ad,'' he said, indicating the paper with an absent wave of his hand, ''was just an added incentive.''

Molly collapsed back in her chair with a long sigh. ''Good grief.''

He smiled. ''If it makes you feel better, I admit I

should have dealt with this differently. I apologize for not talking to you about it sooner.''

"We both could have avoided a lot of embarrassment,'' she said.

"Probably. But now, I'm interested in damage control. Do we have a deal, Molly?''

She tapped one finger in absent agitation on her knee. "What if people don't buy it?''

"Leave that to me,'' he assured her. "I'm not worried.''

"And all I have to do is be seen in public with you—every now and then?''

"You're not currently involved with anyone, are you?'' he probed.

She shook her head. "No.''

"Then it won't be a problem. I'll try not to bore you.''

Molly looked stunned, then burst into laughter. "Are you kidding? Geez, Sam, you irritate me, you annoy me, you frustrate me, and you challenge me. But you *never* bore me!''

"I talk too much about my business.''

"In case you haven't noticed, so do I. And since your business and my business are the same business, I doubt that's a concern.''

Sam felt better than he had in weeks. Satisfaction settled firmly into his bones as he contemplated the future. "Then go to the meeting with me,'' he urged. "We'll have lunch afterwards, and then come back to the office around three. You can explain things in the newsroom, and tonight, we'll have dinner. Everyone will assume that since the cat's finally out of the bag, we have decided to go public with our relationship." He shrugged slightly. "If you want, I'll even take responsibility for keeping our relationship secret until now. People will simply believe that you got angry at me for insisting on privacy, and that you ran the ad to force my hand."

"It's so ridiculous," she conceded, "it might work."

"It'll work. Have you read the tabloids lately? People like ridiculous stories. It's human nature."

She frowned slightly as she thought it over. Sam liked the way Molly looked when she concentrated. The harder she concentrated on something, the more she worried the tip of her tongue between her teeth. He found it unexpectedly sexy. "What if we find out we really can't get along—that all we do after hours is fight like we do now? Then what?"

Sam recognized a wary concession in the question. "We'll end it," he stated flatly. "The only thing I ask is that we end it quietly." His gaze dropped to the classified section of the paper on his desk. "I don't like spectacles."

Molly winced. "After seeing that ad this morning, I don't either."

"Then we have a deal?"

She visibly wavered. "What about my family? What do I tell them?"

Sam began to relax. He might not know much about romancing women—women, Sam found, usually chased *him*—but he knew a lot about making deals. Anticipating questions that might arise was key to a successful negotiation. And he'd anticipated this one from Molly. Nobody who lived in Payne more than a few days could help noticing the closeness of the large Flynn clan. Molly's father owned a popular downtown restaurant where two of his sons-in-law worked with him. And all five of the Flynn daughters still lived in town. One was a teacher. Another was a lawyer. Two were stay-at-home moms. And then there was Molly. The only one of the five not yet married, she was widely known as the family rebel. Molly was the youngest of the girls. She was tight with her sisters and wouldn't be comfortable deceiving them.

Sam met her gaze across the desk. "Tell them the truth," he said. "Tell them that we met here. That sparks flew. That we determined we had some mutual interests, and that we've decided to explore them to see where they lead us."

Molly gave him a blank look, then burst into laughter. "They're not going to believe that."

Irritated by her casual dismissal, Sam frowned. "Why not?"

"Because, in a million years I wouldn't say something like 'we decided to explore our mutual interests.' Geez, Sam, I've never *decided* to get involved in a relationship in my life." She shook her head. "I'm more the jerk-open-the-door-and-run-on-in type. I hurtle into relationships. I don't decide myself into them."

He understood her point. Yet, one of the things that fascinated him about Molly was that he didn't find her impulsiveness annoying. He'd known women he would have called impulsive, and for the most part, he'd found them flaky and irritating. But Molly seemed to have an energy, a certain vim—that made everything she did seem engaging and enticing.

"What would you like to tell them?" Sam asked carefully.

Molly worried her lower lip between her teeth for a few seconds. "I don't want to lie."

"I can understand that."

"But you also have to understand— I don't know—I guess I'll make it up as I go along."

"May I assume, then, that you agree?" he asked quietly.

Molly hesitated a moment longer, then nodded. Standing, she extended her hand. "We have a deal, Mr. Reed."

He folded her hand in his and took the opportunity to skim his thumb over the pulse in her wrist. "I think you'd better start calling me Sam." He glanced at his watch. "And we'd better get moving. I don't want to be late for this meeting."

## Chapter Three

Sam slid a glance at Molly as she sat beside him in the conference room of the mayor's office. She was studying a sheaf of papers the mayor's secretary had handed Sam when they'd arrived for the meeting. And she was worrying her tongue between her teeth again.

He watched her tuning out the nasal voice of the management contractor the town had hired to oversee the development of a rail, air, and shipping distribution hub. If successfully built and managed, this hub could soon triple the size of the small town of Payne.

But Sam had several suspicions about the project, especially about the management firm and the bidding process. He knew from editorial meetings that Molly shared his suspicions. Reviewing the public documents himself, he had thus far turned up nothing. Molly had been badgering him for an assignment for weeks, but he'd evaded her, primarily because he didn't want to send up warning flags for the mayor's office.

There wasn't an influential citizen in Payne who didn't understand that Molly was no ordinary small-town journalist. If the mayor had something to hide, he sure wouldn't want Molly looking for it. And the wary glance Sam had gotten from the mayor's assistant when he and Molly arrived for the meeting had confirmed his suspicions.

"Mr. Reed," the young woman had said, studying Molly with a sharp gaze. "The mayor didn't mention you were bringing anyone." She had tipped her head toward Molly. "Hello, Molly."

"Jean," Molly had said coolly. She'd slipped her hands into the back pockets of her jeans. Sam could never figure out how Molly managed to look professional and sophisticated in jeans and a sweatshirt—which appeared to be her attire of choice. The only time he'd seen her in a dress was the day she'd had to attend a midday funeral. She'd come to work wearing a dark brown dress that did something incredible to her figure and her coloring. The hem had skimmed her knees, and though the dress itself was nothing other than sedate, it didn't look sedate on Molly.

He'd had a hard time concentrating that morning at the editorial meeting. She'd kept crossing her legs, and he'd kept staring at the way her shapely legs tapered down to a pair of conservative heels. He'd asked himself repeatedly what the hell he was thinking. Sam had decided there was a very good reason for Molly to stay in jeans and sneakers. The sedate brown dress had been bad enough. Anything more seductive might do him in.

When they'd arrived at the town offices, Molly had looked squarely at the mayor's assistant and waited for Sam to explain her presence at the meeting. Sam had seized the opportunity. "Molly and I have lunch plans,'' he had said casually. ''I figured if she came with me to the meeting, we could just leave from here.''

Jean's perfectly shaped brows had disappeared beneath the sweep of hair over her forehead. ''I see,'' she said. ''Well, I suppose I could ask—''

''I'm sure Fred won't mind,'' Sam had insisted, referring to the mayor. ''This is just an informational meeting, isn't it?''

Jean had hesitated slightly. ''Yes.''

Sam had taken the folder of briefing papers from her and handed it to Molly. ''Then I'm sure there's no problem.''

Left with no reasonable rebuttal, Jean had shown them into the conference room.

As usual, Sam had been the first to arrive. He took a seat to the right of the mayor's designated chair at the head of the table. Molly had waved the folder at him with a dry grin. ''You're good, Sam.''

Sam had accepted the throaty compliment with a clench in his gut. He was looking forward to hearing her tell him that under more intimate, and more private, circumstances. ''I figured you were going to make them nervous. That's the main reason I didn't want you looking into this before.''

She'd seemed surprised. ''You suspect something, too?''

''For weeks,'' he'd confirmed.

''You could have just told me that, you know.''

At the note of irritation in her voice, Sam had shrugged. ''I wasn't ready.''

He sensed Molly struggling with frustration. ''You know what your problem is, Sam?''

"No, but I assure you plenty of people have tried to figure it out."

She ignored that. Her eyes were sparkling. He'd noticed weeks ago that Molly's eyes always sparkled in proportion to her passion. He felt another clench in his gut as he considered what she'd look like with her hair rumpled and her face flushed in the aftermath of passion. "Your problem," Molly said pointedly, "is that you don't trust people. Life's more rewarding when you trust people."

"I've heard that," he said noncommittally. He'd indicated the seat across from him to the mayor's left. "Why don't you sit over there? That way, we can see all the faces and compare notes later."

"Divide and conquer?" She'd made her way to the other side of the table.

"Something like that."

Molly had nodded thoughtfully. "How nervous do you think it'll make the mayor if I study these briefings during the meeting?"

"Extremely," he'd assured her.

"That's what I think. You listen, I'll read."

Now, an hour later, true to her word, Molly had said nothing since greeting the mayor, the director of development and public works, and the lawyers and the front man for the management firm. She'd settled into her chair and begun to read systematically through the information in the folder.

The mayor, Sam noted, continued to slide nervous glances in her direction. The tip of Molly's tongue had appeared between her teeth about thirty minutes ago. She'd started flipping back and forth between pages in the folder as if comparing information. Sam observed one of the development lawyers thumping his pencil on the conference table in obvious agitation.

"I really just wanted to bring you up to speed, Sam," Mayor Fred Cobell told him. "It's like I told you in the beginning, this project is going to mean a lot to the future of Payne."

"Without a doubt," Sam agreed.

Ed Newbury, the Director of Transportation and Public Works, nodded avidly. "And the *Sentinel* can have a huge influence on how people perceive it."

Sam saw Molly bristle. He steepled his fingers beneath his chin. "We have every intention on reporting about the phases of the project," he assured them.

The development firm's spokesman laughed nervously. "Positively, I hope."

Molly gave him a chilly look. "We report the news, Mr. Patterson. It doesn't matter whether it's good news or bad news, we just tell the story."

"Now, Molly," Fred Cobell said, patting the table in front of her, "don't get your reporter instincts in a twist. Nobody's asking for any favors here."

"I'm glad to hear that," she told him.

The mayor looked at Sam. "However," he said, "you know as well as I do that a local news outlet can seriously influence how citizens feel about a certain project."

"No doubt," Sam agreed.

"And I'd be lying if I said I didn't hope that the *Sentinel* would help the people of Payne see how important this project is to our community."

Sam didn't like Fred Cobell. He'd decided that the first day he'd met the man. Cobell had a clammy handshake. In fifteen years of business, Sam had never met a trustworthy man with a clammy handshake.

And subsequent meetings and conversations had confirmed his first impression of Cobell as a small-town politician with big-city aspirations and an over-developed love of wealth and power.

Now, Sam met Cobell's probing gaze with a cool look. "I have every intention of keeping the community informed about the benefits," he assured Cobell. From the corner of his eye, Sam detected Molly's sharp frown. "The *Sentinel* has always been committed to serving this community."

Cobell searched Sam's expression for long seconds, then nodded, apparently reassured. "I'm glad to hear that, Sam. I'm sure you'll find that maintaining a good relationship with our office will make your job in Payne a little easier."

Sam gritted his teeth against the urge to tell Cobell he had a seriously overinflated impression of his own importance if he thought his influence and opinion even registered on Sam's radar. "I'm going to do the job Carl asked me here to do," he stated flatly. "The *Sentinel* needs some restructuring, but I'm sure we can maintain its credibility in this community."

The mayor nodded. "Sure, sure. Payne has always relied on the *Sentinel* for important community news. I'm sure your cooperation with us is going to enhance that reputation."

Sam shrugged. "We'll see."

"I'm sure we will," Cobell assured him. He looked at the other two men in the room. "I'm certainly glad we had this meeting."

"Me, too," Patterson agreed. He pulled on his collar. "I think this is going to be good for all of us."

Cobell returned his gaze to Sam. "I'm sure Jean can answer any other questions you might have. I'll make my staff available to the *Sentinel* for any information you might need."

Sam recognized the dismissal. He glanced at Molly. Her color had heightened slightly, and her eyes glistened. She pressed her lips tightly together. Sam sensed that her annoyance at Cobell's condescension was surpassed only by her annoyance with him for playing the unfolding story so close to his chest.

He couldn't blame her, either. He'd been tough on her for the past few weeks, and undoubtedly deserved the blistering lecture he'd get when they left the mayor's office.

He rose to leave. "I'm sure you will, Fred. Thanks." He gestured at Molly. "Now, if we're through, Molly and I have lunch plans."

Cobell looked quickly from Sam to Molly and back again, his gaze speculative. "I see," he said carefully. He grinned broadly at Sam. "I see."

Sam squashed his irritation while he and Molly said their goodbyes and made their way through the mayor's outer office. As he punched the down button in the elevator he uttered a dark curse that succinctly summed up his opinion of Fred Cobell, a word which questioned the mayor's lack of paternal heritage. Molly shot him a quick look. "I'm surprised."

"You've never heard me swear before?" he asked flatly, still trying to shake his lingering foul mood.

"Funny, Sam," she said. "What I meant was, I

was a little surprised to hear you calling him names in the elevator when you seemed awfully ready to give him what he wanted by the time he wrapped up the meeting.''

"Then you don't know me very well," he said as the elevator glided to a stop at the ground floor. He pinned her with a sharp look. "We'll discuss this in the car," he stated. "I don't want to be overheard."

TWENTY MINUTES LATER, Molly drummed her fingers on the table of Stingy Eddy's diner and admitted a reluctant, but growing admiration for Sam Reed. At least, she thought wryly, since she'd admitted to herself that she found him incredibly attractive, she could take comfort in the fact that she had exceptionally good taste. He'd played Fred Cobell, she'd realized during the meeting, but the extent of Sam's insight into the matter still surprised her as he'd explained his suspicions about the development project in the short ride to the restaurant. "How long have you known this?" she pressed him now.

Sam shrugged. "Something smelled bad right from the beginning." He took a long sip of water and settled down in the banquette. His lazy grace, Molly noted, made him seem at home in any setting—from the mayor's office to the greasy spoon. "I think Cobell is one of those small town politicians who lets power and money go to his head."

"He's been mayor for fifteen years," Molly said. "I don't think he started out wanting to be a career politician—"

"But he changed his mind."

She shrugged. "What does the retired mayor of a

small town do except marshal a few parades now and then?'' She mentally reviewed the reports she'd scanned during the meeting. ''I find it hard to believe that Cobell would actually do anything illegal, though.''

''Not in a place like Payne?''

She frowned at him. He had a way of talking about her small community that made her bristle. It had been one of the first things she'd noticed when he arrived at the *Sentinel*. Sure, Payne might not have the cosmopolitan atmosphere of Boston, but the town had a special quality that Molly found both charming and comforting. ''Look, Sam, small towns may not be your personal cup of tea, but they provide a certain security for their citizens. Payne is a community. It's still the kind of community where you don't have to lock your doors and look over your shoulder when you walk down the street at night. Some people like that.''

''Just an observation, Molly. Not a criticism.''

She exhaled an exasperated sigh. ''Do you know that every time you talk about the community you sound condescending?''

He looked surprised. ''I do?''

She nodded. ''Yes. You seem to think we're beneath your standards—''

''I do not.''

She gave him a pointed look. ''*Now* who's interrupting?''

Sam frowned. ''I do *not* think the people of Payne are beneath my standards.''

''You sound like you do.''

His face was a mask of concentration and, unless

she missed her guess, genuine concern, as he thought about her statement. "Why do you say that?" he asked.

"It's the way you talk about us, about our lives." She paused as she weighed the wisdom of her next statement. "As if you think we're trivial."

He frowned. "You're serious?"

"Maybe we're not the kind of town that makes national news, but we're good, solid people. We deserve more than your contempt."

He nodded, visibly thoughtful. "I agree. I never meant to communicate contempt."

She shrugged. "Maybe not, but it would help if you actually involved yourself in what goes on around here."

"How so?"

Molly took a deep breath, ignoring the voice in her head that said she'd clearly lost her mind. "What are your plans for the weekend?" she asked, knowing full well that Sam left town every Friday afternoon. Most of the *Sentinel* staff knew he lived in a residential hotel outside Payne and that he commuted home to Boston on weekends. The fact that he'd made no pretense of the strictly temporary nature of his stay had chafed.

"I have some plans on the coast."

She could well imagine. The Reed clan's connection to the Massachusetts coastline was legendary. Sam's brother owned a large home in Rockport, and his sister had indulged in several infamous, high-profile retreats in trendy Martha's Vineyard. "The duck races are Saturday," she reminded him.

His lips twitched. "How could I forget?"

Irritated, Molly gave him a sharp look. "You see? That's exactly what I'm talking about. So what if the duck races aren't the Indianapolis 500? The festival is the biggest event of the year in Payne. Even if you think it's corny, you don't have to be so smug."

Sam shook his head, his expression rueful. "Molly—I was serious. How could I forget the duck races when you spent last week's editorial meeting arguing with me about my plans for the coverage?"

She, too, remembered the heated meeting. Sam had decided to do away with the traditional coverage of the festival in favor of a background piece that explored the original vision of Howard Edgington, founder of the event and the primary endower of the scholarship program that encouraged Payne High School students to participate. "People are going to miss the recap," Molly told him, now. "They look forward to it."

"Then why don't the last three years' business stats show an increase in sales the Monday morning after?"

Irritated, Molly glared at him. "Despite what you might think, Sam, I'm probably the biggest proponent on staff of making changes to the *Sentinel* if that's what it takes to save it."

"Is that why you've been harassing me in meetings since the day I got here?" he drawled.

"I don't harass," she stated. At his dry look, she shook her head. "I don't. I just argue."

Sam laughed. "Point well taken."

"And it might surprise you that I want to fix the problems, too, but I don't think we have to do away with the *Sentinel*'s character to do that."

"Neither do I," he assured her.

"Then why are you giving me grief about the duck races coverage?"

"Your way won't sell papers. My way will."

Molly gritted her teeth. "Look, Sam, I'll grant you that the festival is a little quirky. Fine, the duck races won't stand up to Paul Revere Days in Boston. Maybe they won't make the national registry of historic events, or get a write-up in *Town & Country,* but the duck races are ours." She gave him a hard look. "And we *like* them, Sam. There's nothing wrong with that."

"I know."

"The teenagers who compete in the scholarship contest work toward this all year—sometimes for longer than a year. They deserve better than a two-line mention in the community newspaper for their accomplishments."

"Are you listening to yourself?" he asked.

"Yes. And that's exactly my point. You can't believe I feel this passionately about ducks."

"Sure I can. You feel passionately about everything." He paused. "Especially everything about Payne."

She let that pass. "As hard as it may be for you to believe, there are some people in this world who enjoy the quaintness of things like duck races."

"For your information, I happen to be one of those people."

Molly thought she detected a slightly bitter note in his voice, but she pressed on. "You just don't think they're worthy of print coverage."

"I think that when everyone in the town attends

the festival, a recap isn't going to sell any papers—except maybe to the family of the scholarship winner. But I also think there are enough new people in Payne that covering the history of the event and its founder is both relevant and marketable.''

''Maybe,'' she conceded, ''but the point isn't about circulation—''

''It's always about circulation,'' Sam replied.

Molly rolled her eyes. ''We're talking about you and this town—not the paper. Whether or not your way will sell more papers doesn't change the fact that you, yourself, said you're having trouble getting people to accept you.''

He seemed to think that over. ''And you believe it's because I changed the coverage of the duck races?''

''No, Sam,'' she said with strained patience. ''I think it's because you handed down your decision without even discussing it with the editorial staff.''

''You're probably right,'' he said. ''I don't have a lot of patience with the whining that goes on in those meetings. It's mostly counterproductive.''

''I don't think they consider their creative input whining,'' she replied sharply.

''Yours isn't,'' he concurred. ''You actually seem to have thought through your proposals before you field them.''

''Thanks.''

If Sam noticed her sarcasm, he didn't comment. ''But except for Daniel Constega, the rest of them just like to complain.''

Molly closed her eyes in frustration. ''That's exactly what I mean, Sam.''

"What?"

She looked at him again. "You can't simply denigrate people's work styles because they don't happen to be the same as yours. Carl didn't run the paper the way you do. The writers are used to having a lot of input."

"Which is why," he pointed out, "the *Sentinel* has covered the duck races the same way every year for a decade."

"People like it. Traditions have their place."

He hesitated. "You're probably right."

Surprised, Molly studied him through narrowed eyes. "Are you agreeing with me?"

"It looks like it."

"My God. We might have to declare a municipal holiday."

He regarded her with a definite sparkle in his gray eyes. "Maybe we could call it 'Duck Day.'"

"Don't start that again," she said tartly, still chafing with remembered frustration at his apparent snobbery.

"I'm not belittling the ducks—or the teenagers who race them."

"Just because they don't win something prestigious like a scholarship to Harvard doesn't mean they don't work hard and accomplish something significant."

"I agree."

"A lot of teenagers don't have the sense of responsibility or commitment to spend an entire year working toward something."

"True."

She glared at him. "What are you trying to pull, Sam?"

"Pull?"

"You *never* agree with me. In all the weeks that you've been here, can you name one time when you've agreed with me?"

He nodded. "Actually, I agree with you more than you know."

Exasperated, Molly blew an auburn curl off her forehead. "In *public?* Can you think of one time you've agreed with me in public?"

"No," he said bluntly. "I can't."

"And now you've done it, what, four times since we sat down?"

"Are you complaining?"

"I feel like I'm in the twilight zone."

"Because you're determined to find something about me you can't stand?"

"There's plenty about you I can't stand," she assured him. "Want a list?"

That made him laugh. She had to remember to stop giving him reasons to laugh. Every time she heard that warm, rich chuckle, it made her stomach flip. "No, I'll pass," he said.

*Too bad,* Molly thought. She would probably benefit from the opportunity to remind herself of his flaws. As usual, she was tumbling fast down the rabbit hole of infatuation with a man who'd made his "strictly temporary" intentions very clear. They had a business arrangement, he'd said. A mutually beneficial partnership. If she had a brain in her head, she'd remember that. She took a fortifying breath. "Rats."

He laughed again. "You're dying to tell me, aren't you?"

"I've been dying to tell you since you got here. I

was actually kind of hoping you'd fire me this morning."

"License to vent?"

"Sure. Wouldn't you relish the opportunity if you were me?"

"Absolutely," he assured her. "To be perfectly frank, I've been marveling at your self-control for weeks. I was sort of wondering when you were going to crack."

*Good Lord,* she thought, was he actually teasing her? Until this morning, she'd have sworn that Sam Reed had been born with no sense of humor and was personality-challenged. "Friday," she told him. "I cracked on Friday."

A devilish smile played at the corner of his mouth. "Yeah, I guess you did."

Molly blew a stray curl off her forehead as she mentally chided herself for the way her heart accelerated at the sight of his dimple. "And since you *did* ask for my help in getting the people of Payne to accept you, then you've got to believe me when I tell you that you sound as if you think we're beneath you."

He frowned again. "That's not true."

"So, fine. You'd better figure out how to communicate that."

"Would it help if I told you I arranged to match the Duck Foundation's grant and give the scholarship winner an additional two thousand dollars?"

Her eyes widened. "Are you serious?"

"Yes." He spread his hands on the table. "I have great admiration for any kid who's willing to work that hard to get a college education—no matter what the accomplishment. It shows determination, responsibility and commitment. I think that should be rewarded.''

"Did you tell anyone about this?" she pressed.

"No. Generosity tends to make people hostile."

His eyes took on a sad look that made Molly wonder who had burned Sam for his generous nature. "That's an interesting way of looking at the world," she said.

"People are suspicious of generosity. They think you want something in return."

"Probably because most people do."

He shrugged. "It may be better to give than receive, but receiving takes humility. People don't like it."

Molly studied him closely. "How did you come by that conclusion, Sam?"

He waved a hand in dismissal. "Long story. I'll tell you later." The sad look disappeared from his eyes. Molly felt she'd just let a rare opportunity slip from her fingers. "So do you think my reputation is too far gone for me to redeem myself with the citizens of Payne?"

"I don't think—"

"The paper could hold a ceremony. We could crown the scholarship winner the duck king or something." Tiny lines appeared at the corner of his eyes. Molly was beginning to recognize them as the sure indicator that Sam was up to mischief. She watched him for a moment, intrigued. There had been something in his gaze just a moment ago, and he'd chased it away with this teasing look. Interesting, she thought, *I wonder why I've taken so long to observe how many layers there are to this man.*

"The duck king?" she finally prompted.

"With an entire duck court. We'd give out duck calls. We'd wear duck shoes."

"Sam—"

"Local restaurants could serve duck-related foods."

"Duck-related foods?"

"Duck à l'orange. Duck soup. Roast duck." She glared at him. "Cheese and quackers."

His expression was so serious, it took her a moment to catch the pun. Despite herself, Molly laughed. She wadded up her napkin and tossed it at him. "You're impossible."

He caught the napkin in one hand. "So I've heard." Sam pinned her with a close look.

Molly returned the look. "And speaking of impossible, why did you wait until today to let me in on your plans for the transportation story?"

"You saw what happened at the meeting—"

"Everyone was shocked that you and I could be in the same room without killing one another."

His mouth kicked up at the corners. "You didn't let me finish."

She scowled. "Well, they were."

"You and I might be legendary around the *Sentinel* office, but I don't think most of Payne is talking about the fact that we've been hashing it out in editorial meetings."

"I think you seriously underestimate the power of small-town gossip."

"Maybe, but what I was going to say was that you

have a reputation for being Carl's go-to reporter. If there's a serious story to be written, you're on it.''

"Because I'm the best writer he has," she pointed out.

"Yes," Sam concurred.

Molly experienced a rush of endorphins at his affirmation. She was starting to feel like an adolescent and she hated it. "And," Sam continued, "if Cobell had known or suspected that I had you looking into the project, he wouldn't have been as forthcoming with information."

That, she admitted, was probably true. "You insinuated to the mayor that you'd cooperate with his PR campaign to sell the project."

"I insinuated," he told her. "I didn't actually promise him anything."

"Maybe, but he's expecting—"

"I couldn't care less what he's expecting." He cradled his hands together and leaned toward her. "I've let Cobell get comfortable with me for a reason. Now it's time to start shaking him up a little. My brother, Ben, says that if you want to know about a person's character, just shake them up and see what comes out."

Molly smiled. "Good advice."

"And now that I have Cobell where I want him— which is pretty far out on a limb—I'm ready to start shaking the tree a little."

"That makes sense."

"And the opportunity to explore stories like this are exactly the reason I want to help Carl save the *Sentinel*. If we can make the paper profitable with a few innovations—"

"Like advice columns and coupons?" she said dryly.

"You may not like them, but yes, features like that are consistently profitable in smaller market publications."

"The *Sentinel* is a serious paper."

"And it's going to be seriously out of business if we can't increase the readership."

"I know," she insisted. "It's just that I can't believe there isn't a better way to do it than diluting the paper's journalistic edge."

"Have you been listening to anything I've said over the past few weeks?"

"Of course—"

He held up a hand. "I have no intention of taking the edge off the *Sentinel*'s content."

"But—" At his knowing look, she swallowed her instincts and said reluctantly, "Go ahead."

"Just because I've introduced a few regular features doesn't mean the paper won't have plenty of room for solid journalism. I've been waiting for the right story."

"Like the transportation project."

"The time is right," he said. "I didn't want to alert Cobell that I was going to look into this, but in retrospect, I could have handled things differently."

"Carl ran an open forum," she told him. "We're not used to being in the dark. It makes us feel that you don't trust us."

"Maybe I just wanted to know how hard I could push before you pushed back."

"Are you *apologizing* to me?" she asked, slightly incredulous.

"Don't jump to conclusions," he muttered.

Molly searched his expression, but found nothing. Their waitress chose that moment to deliver their food. "Hey, Molly," she said as she set the plates down. "Everything going okay?"

Molly had known Amanda Freeman since she'd talked Stingy Eddy into giving Amanda her job as a waitress. Molly had met her at the bus station while researching a story on the financial hardships of single mothers and befriended her. At the time, Amanda had been taking odd jobs, but was on the verge of turning to prostitution to feed her young daughter. With Molly's encouragement, she'd gotten help to kick her drug habit and was now making a productive living for herself and her child. "Sure, Mandy," Molly told her. She indicated Sam with a wave of her hand. "Have you met Sam Reed?"

Mandy wiped her hands on her apron, then extended one to Sam. "You the guy who's taken over the paper?"

"I'm helping Carl Morgan make some adjustments to the *Sentinel*," Sam clarified.

Mandy looked at Molly. "This the fella from the ad?"

Molly cringed. "Yes."

Mandy gave her a speculative look, then glanced at Sam. A broad smile accompanied the knowing wink she shot Molly's way. "I see," she said carefully. She placed their glasses on the table, then looked at Sam again. "Anything else?" she asked propping her tray on her hip.

He glanced at Molly, then shook his head. "No, thanks. I think that'll do it."

"Okay. I'll be back to check on you in a minute." She tapped Molly's shoulder as she headed back to the kitchen. "You go, girl," she whispered.

Molly groaned and dropped her head into her hands. "Oh, God."

Sam picked up his spoon and twirled it between his fingers. "That wasn't so bad," he told her.

"Speak for yourself."

Sam laughed. "Believe me, if you could have heard my sister this morning, you'd know I've taken my share of hits over this."

Molly gave him an apologetic look. "I really am sorry, Sam. I never meant for this to happen."

He shrugged, but didn't respond. Instead, he turned his attention back to the story. "No matter what mistakes I have made in handling this, I do think the time is right." He pinned her with a knowing look. "And I want you to write the story."

"I won't promise not to make Fred Cobell angry with the *Sentinel,* or with you."

He grinned at her. "I wouldn't expect such a promise, Molly."

She thought for a minute. "You know, Sam, now that I think about it, one of the reasons you've been successful with Cobell is the same reason you've had trouble getting the staff to buy into your plans for the paper."

"How do you mean?"

"Well, Cobell is attracted to the fact that you're from the Boston financial world. The fact that you're Edward Reed's son doesn't hurt either."

"I can see that. But if you're serious about making

Cobell nervous, then I think now is the time for your coming-out party.''

''Now?'' Molly waved a hand in annoyance. ''This is exactly what I'm talking about, Sam. You say you don't understand why you're having trouble getting people to trust you, but you're planning to leave town instead of attending the festival next weekend. And without even going, you've already made up your mind about the event coverage.''

''I have my reasons.''

Molly stubbornly held his gaze. ''It doesn't look good,'' she told him. ''It makes you seem like a snob.''

He nodded thoughtfully. ''I can see that, and I think you're right. I should go.''

His easy concession made her suspicious. ''Just like that? You changed your mind?''

''Sure. Half the battle to save the *Sentinel* is changing Payne's perceptions of what they want in a paper and its publisher. I asked you to help me with that. This is your advice, and I'm going to take it.''

''You're smarter than I thought,'' she told him.

Sam laughed. ''I promise not to take that personally.''

''I meant it personally.''

His grin didn't falter. Molly resisted the urge to press a palm against her stomach, where butterflies had been congregating all morning. Sam continued, ''Besides, I've never attended a duck race. It might be entertaining.''

''It's a small-town festival,'' she told him. ''Most people find it charming.''

"I imagine they do." He grinned at her. "I'm looking forward to experiencing it with you."

She stilled, sensing she'd just walked into a trap. "With me?"

"Of course. It's the biggest event of the year. You said so yourself. Besides, you will have all day to convince me that the duck races deserve front-page coverage."

"All day?" she hedged.

"You will have my undivided attention for your cause."

"And everyone in town will see us together," she guessed.

"Even better," Sam assured her.

He'd trapped her neatly. Sam was smart enough to know that the entire population of Payne, Massachusetts, and its neighboring townships would be at the festival that weekend. If he and Molly appeared together, it would fuel the speculation she'd already started with the personal ad.

And the legendary Flynn "pluck" wasn't the only thing Aunt Ida extolled. Flynns also took their licks and faced the consequences of their actions. Molly faced the grim reality that she'd just decided to plunge headfirst into the Payne gossip mill and nodded. "Okay, Sam, I'll do it." At his look of triumph, she added, "but only for the ducks."

# Chapter Four

"Okay, Molly." Cindy pressed a cup of iced coffee into her hand at 4:30 that afternoon in her office. "I'm dying here."

Molly cringed. This was the part of her bargain with Sam that she'd feared. But at least she got to face her friends at the paper before she had to tell her family. It was a chance to brush up on her technique before she got the inquisition from her sisters. The stack of pink messages on her desk from the Flynn clan had not escaped her attention. "He...let me keep my job," she told Cindy carefully.

Cindy glanced meaningfully at the pile of research notes Molly had brought from the Office of Public Documents. "That's obvious."

Molly had been relieved at the excuse of the development story to spend the better part of the day away from the office. Even the musty environs of City Hall were more desirable than the close confines and prying eyes of the newsroom. "It was just a misunderstanding." She rolled a pencil between her thumb and index finger and took a long sip of her drink.

Cindy's eyebrows arched. "It didn't look like

much of a misunderstanding when the two of you breezed through here this morning.'' She flicked the daisy in Molly's pencil cup with a manicured fingernail. "You gotta admit, after the last few weeks of watching the two of you nearly kill each other in meetings, this is a little surprising.''

Molly drew a steadying breath. "Passion has many forms," she replied softly. Sam had said so himself.

"So you *are* involved with him." Cindy's expression turned triumphant. "I knew it. I've known it for weeks, actually. There's no way there were so many sparks between you two—unless something was going on.''

Score one for Sam, Molly thought wryly. He'd been right when he'd said that people saw what they wanted to see. She gave Cindy a slight smile. "Well, the cat's out of the bag now, I guess.''

Cindy leaned closer to her. "So, um, I don't suppose I can get you to tell me what he's like, you know, in the sack? I've been wondering for weeks.''

Molly stifled a groan. "Cin—"

"Yeah, yeah, I know." The blonde shook her head. "You're not the type to talk about something like that." She regarded Molly with pursed lips. "Come to think of it, I've known you, what, six years?''

"About.''

"And in six years, I don't think I've ever heard you gossip about your love life." Cindy laughed lightly. "But then—and don't take this the wrong way—but the men you've been involved with, well, it didn't seem like there was a lot to tell.''

"I date nice guys," Molly insisted.

"Exactly my point." Cindy gave her a shrewd

look. "In my experience, there's not a whole lot to tell when you're involved with a nice guy."

Despite herself, Molly smiled. There was something oddly endearing about Cindy's flightiness. She didn't seem to mind that most people mistook her breezy nature for lack of intelligence. In fact, Cindy's facade masked a sharp mind and quick wit Molly had come to admire. "Maybe I'm just not the tell-all type," she quipped.

"That—or," Cindy frowned slightly, "you're one of those search-and-rescue kind of women."

"Search and rescue?"

"Sure. You know the type. You seek out hurting men, drag them from the quagmire, patch 'em up, and send them on their way."

Molly fought the urge to wince. "I don't think—"

"Come on, Molly, how many guys have you dated and then fixed up with other friends?"

"A few," she hedged.

"A lot." Cindy tapped one long fingernail on Molly's desk. "I've seen 'em tramp through here. Lord, girl, you sure know how to pick 'em."

"Just because I like respectable—"

"Boring," Cindy insisted. "You like boring guys."

"They're not boring." Molly had a sneaking suspicion that she was beginning to sound defensive.

"Come to think of it," Cindy continued, "that's probably why I didn't pick up on this thing with you and Reed. He's just not your usual type."

"That's an understatement."

"I never really understood that about you," Cindy continued, studying her closely. "You've got a lot to work with there. That hair," she rolled her eyes, "there was a time when I would have killed for hair like yours."

"That's only because you've never actually *had* red hair," Molly assured her. She'd given up fighting with her mop of dark red curls years ago. She was the only one of the five Flynn girls with her father's red hair and freckles.

"Yeah, well, men find it sexy. Take my word for it."

That made Molly laugh. "Come on, Cin, you're the one with the long platinum hair. Don't tell me guys don't like that."

Cindy's eyes darted beyond Molly's shoulder toward the elevator. "Depends on the guy, I suppose," she said.

Molly followed the direction of Cindy's gaze to find Sam Reed walking purposefully toward her, his jacket tossed casually over his shoulder, his white shirt and black suspenders making his chest look impossibly broad. *Drat,* she thought. She'd hoped her sudden realization of his personal charisma had been a passing phase brought on by the stress of the morning and the bizarre circumstances in which she now found herself. If she could, she'd rethink her decision to take his offer and keep her job. "But Flynns," her father would say, "always keep their word." And for better or worse, Molly had made a bargain.

A bargain that had her pulse racing every time she got too close to Sam. Sam, the world-traveled, high-powered business mogul, who couldn't possibly find life in a small town like Payne other than mindnumbingly tedious. Molly figured there'd never been a more unlikely match than she and Sam. Passion was one thing, but once it burned down to a slow fire, there just wasn't enough in Molly Flynn's world to keep a man like Sam Reed interested.

With a weary sigh, she pushed the folder with her notes from the document office into her top desk drawer, turned the key, and met Cindy's gaze again. "I've got to go."

Cindy nodded. "We can finish tomorrow." She glanced at Sam who was nearing Molly's desk. "Hi, Mr. Reed."

Sam nodded casually. "Hello." He placed one hand on Molly's shoulder. "Ready, babe?"

Molly fought the urge to groan out loud. *Babe.* Good God. Had he really called her babe? The fact that Sam managed to say the word without sounding like a lounge lizard annoyed her. And the knowing look in Cindy's eyes told her that the little tidbit about Sam's endearment would be all over the newsroom by morning. With a sinking feeling, Molly reached for her purse. She frowned at Sam. He had the nerve to wink at her. "I'm ready," she announced, swinging her purse over her shoulder as she headed for the door.

THEY WERE HALFWAY ACROSS the parking lot before Sam acknowledged the glare in Molly's eyes. "Something bothering you?"

"Babe?" She gave him an incredulous look. "*Babe?* What the crabnabbits were you thinking?"

He stopped by her car and propped one hip on the passenger door. "Crabnabbits?"

"I *cannot* believe you called me 'babe.' Ugh."

He raised an eyebrow. "Crabnabbits?"

Exasperated, Molly folded her arms across her chest. "My mother didn't let us swear."

His mouth kicked up at the corner. "How many times did you get your mouth washed out with soap?"

"If you must know, I actually learned to like the taste of Ivory." She scowled at him. "And quit changing the subject."

"You're rankled because I called you babe?"

"You could say that."

"Is it the word that annoys you—" he gave her a close look "—or the fact that I said it in front of Cindy?"

Molly visibly gritted her teeth. "Both."

"Fine." He shrugged casually. "I'll cross it off the list of acceptable salutations." Her color, he noted, was rising again. He wondered if she'd blow a gasket if he told her she turned him on when she got angry. "But I can't do anything about Cindy."

"Damn it, Sam—"

"I thought you weren't supposed to swear."

Her eyes closed slowly. Sam could hear her counting to ten beneath her breath. When she looked at him again, her expression was probing and intent. "Do you enjoy irritating me?" she asked softly.

He glanced quickly at the *Sentinel* building where several employees were standing in the exit watching the exchange with rapt curiosity. "Honestly?" he asked.

Molly nodded. Sam grinned at her. She had a way of making him feel like a mischievous schoolboy. "Yeah. I kind of do."

Her huff was simultaneously exasperated and adorable. "God, you're insufferable."

"You're not the first woman to tell me that."

"What in the world made you think we could make
this work? There isn't a snowball's chance in Florida
that people are going to believe you and I are anything but hostile."

This was a question Sam was fully prepared to answer. He'd actually been pondering it for weeks—
ever since the first time Molly had faced off with him
in an editorial meeting and he'd felt a sharp, if surprising, twinge of desire. At first, he'd dismissed it as
a random reaction to her blatant challenge, but as the
days had passed and he'd continued to experience the
various facets of Molly Flynn, the familiar feeling of
banked fire had settled in his gut.

Sam had decided one night while lying in his bed,
staring at the ceiling and thinking about Molly, that
it didn't matter if she wasn't exactly his type. He
wanted her. That was enough.

Looking at her now, he felt a certain satisfaction in
knowing that his instincts had been correct. Molly
wanted him, too. She'd deny it if he asked her, but
the signs were definitely there. Her breath quickened
when she was with him. Her eyes shone a little more
brightly. Her color heightened. And her fingers quivered. That had been the giveaway. He'd noticed it
today at lunch while she'd talked about the duck
races. She'd been gripping her fork and her fingers
had trembled.

One thing Sam knew for sure: trembling fingers
seldom lie. He dropped his coat from his shoulder and
tossed it over one arm so he could brace his hand

against the roof of Molly's car. She was watching him warily, and unless he missed his guess, she was a little rattled by her newfound awareness of him.

The breeze had picked up, and Molly's curls teased the edges of her face, burnished by the late-afternoon sunlight. Sam gently tucked a strand of hair behind her ear, then ran his fingertip along her jaw. Molly's lips parted slightly, and Sam felt his longing spike. He leaned closer, carefully watching the subtle shift of emotion in her eyes. "Because," he said softly. "It's just like I told you. Passion has many forms."

"I don't think—"

He tipped his head toward the building. "We have an audience," he told her.

"I thought that was the whole idea," Molly shot back.

Sam shook his head. "No, Molly. I meant what I said about not playing games. Letting the world think you ran that ad because you were miffed at me was one thing, but when I tell you how much and how often and in how many ways I want you, I'm not going to do it in front of a crowd."

He leaned down and pressed a brief, hard kiss to her lips. Molly was so startled, she didn't react before he'd raised his head. Those tiny lines of mischief had formed at the corner of his eyes again, she noted absently as her head swam slightly. Sam pressed his thumb to her tingling mouth. "I was going to take you to dinner tonight, but there's something I'd like to show you."

Her eyes clouded. "Show me?"

"It's about an hour's drive," he warned. "I'll

make it worth your while. There's a good restaurant there.''

Molly seemed to hesitate. ''Sam—''

He took a step closer, reached for her hand and pulled it to his chest. ''I don't want to argue anymore,'' he said to her. ''Not tonight. Please. Just come with me.''

She searched his face with the painstaking care of a forensic scientist looking for evidence. Sam pressed his advantage. ''Can we just agree to put things behind us for tonight—just to see where it takes us?''

Evidently, she found what she was seeking. ''All right, Sam. Tonight we'll start over.''

MOLLY RAN A HAND over the lovingly polished teak hull. ''It's beautiful,'' she told Sam.

He was watching her in the dim light of the boathouse. They'd made the drive from Payne to a small harbor town south of Rockport where Sam docked the vintage sailboat he'd been restoring for nearly a decade. During the ride, Molly had told him about her afternoon's research. She'd listened attentively while he talked of a deal he and his brother were considering with a major Midwest syndicate. She'd asked questions, made comments, and generally helped him reason through several problems he'd been studying with Ben.

And Sam had admitted to himself that he found her incredibly, intoxicatingly sexy. Though she was still dressed in jeans and a sweatshirt and the day's wind had mussed her hair into a tangle of curls, he doubted he could have found her more seductive if she'd sat next to him in satin-and-lace lingerie. Sam couldn't remember the last time he'd been with a woman who seemed genuinely interested in his life.

Molly did strange things to him. That thought had occurred to him about three weeks ago. He'd realized that his irritability after one of their infamous editorial meeting rows had nothing to do with her challenge to his decision to introduce a second advice column into the *Sentinel*'s daily lineup. During the argument, Molly had insinuated that he had no business deciding what kind and how much advice people in Payne needed, when he had no idea how they lived their lives.

The comment had grated. Sam had never liked being compared to the social elite surrounding Edward Reed. Despite the advantages of Edward's name and fortune, Sam had worked hard for his success. He resented the insinuation that life had come easily to him. He still remembered, and hoped he always would, what his life had been like before Edward Reed took him in.

Watching Molly examine the hull of his boat, he realized why he'd wanted to bring her here. He'd wanted to get her out of Payne where she held the advantage. He'd wanted to show her that there was more to him than she seemed to think. He wanted her alone and in his territory.

Moonlight spilled through the boathouse transom windows, bathing Molly's skin in a soft, luminescent glow. Sam felt his gut twist as he watched her trace a fingertip over a painstakingly polished brass fitting. He wondered what it would feel like to have her fingers touch his skin with that same smooth caress. She gave him a slight smile. "Have you done all the work on this yourself?"

Sam thrust his hands into his pockets to keep from reaching for her. "Mostly," he told her. "I had to take the anchor mechanism to a shop in the Cape to be refitted. And a couple of the fittings are replicas. I'm sticking with those until I can find genuine parts."

The temperature had dropped sharply from the afternoon, and his breath formed a plume of mist in the damp air. He'd taken her to a local seafood restaurant before bringing her to see the boat. He still hadn't fully recovered from watching her eat a two-pound lobster. He'd never known a woman who could make a plastic bib and lobster pick look erotic.

Molly, he was learning, did everything with gusto. Watching her eat had notched his libido into overdrive. By the time he'd unlocked the door and led her inside, he was tingling with anticipation—both for her reaction and for the opportunity to have her completely alone, here in this place where he felt at home and in control. Her delight with the boat made him ache to touch her. He wanted to see that same pleased and satisfied expression on her face after he kissed her. He took a step toward her. "I've been working on it for several years."

"It shows," she assured him. She rubbed the railing with her palm. Sam's mouth went dry as her fingers curled around the sleek wood and squeezed. "You're doing an incredible job."

He wondered if she had any idea what she was doing to him. The way she was physically examining the textures and surfaces of the boat was heating his blood. It was as if he could feel her touching him in the same delicate, probing, exploratory way—and it was having a very graphic and definite effect on him. "It's a labor of love," he told her. Molly stood on tiptoe and peered over the edge of the deck. Sam moved a step closer. One more step, and he could pin her against the hull. His gaze dropped to her rounded bottom. He had to stifle a groan when he pictured it pressed against him.

"Can we go aboard?" she asked him.

Sam pointed to the stepladder. "That way."

As she climbed up the ladder ahead of him, he was treated to the gentle sway of her derriere as she easily climbed the steps. As she swung one leg onto the deck, Sam had a passing thought about Pamela, the woman he'd almost married. She'd tried hard to seduce him. She could have taken lessons from Molly's innocence and exuberance.

Molly looked around with delight. "Oh, Sam," she said, turning to him with a broad smile. "No wonder you love it."

Her expression was genuine and guileless. He'd told her at dinner that he'd salvaged the boat years ago after a particularly harsh winter storm had swept through the coast and devastated some of the smaller fishing communities. He said it had given him a sense of purpose and pride to watch the craft come back to life through his efforts. Sam braced a hand on the jib and swung it gently back and forth. "In my line of work, I get accused of tearing things apart—dismantling important institutions." He held her gaze. "People think Reed Enterprises is only about money and opportunity."

He saw the slight flicker in her expression that told him she understood what he meant. "Sam—I never meant—"

He shook his head. "I hear it a lot," he told her. "You're not the first."

"Change hurts. People don't like it."

He nodded. "But sometimes, change is necessary to stay alive. I like to think of what Ben and I do as effecting change in order to improve the companies that hire us. Sometimes, things have to be cut away." He shrugged. "Sometimes, people have to lose their jobs. It might surprise you to learn that I don't particularly enjoy that part of the business."

"It doesn't." She shook her head. "I never thought you were insensitive—just inflexible."

"Doing what I do is a lot like making this ship seaworthy again. Once, it was a fine vessel. Over time, it lost some of its usefulness. Modernization made ships like this seem outdated and antiquated. But they still have value—you just have to know how to see it."

Molly's hand covered his on the jib. "And you have to be willing to work for it," she said slowly.

"I understand that." He gave her a narrow look. "I do," she insisted. "And I'm not opposed to doing what has to be done to save the *Sentinel*."

He turned his hand so he could grasp hers. Her fingers felt soft and supple. He liked her calluses. Molly wasn't afraid to get her hands a little dirty. He idly rubbed his thumb over a rough spot on the outside edge of her middle finger. It was a pencil callus—and Sam suspected Molly had had it most of her life. "I see the *Sentinel*," he said, "as a worthy and fine institution. And not just because Carl is my friend, either. In some ways, smaller market papers are better poised for certain stories—''

''Like the transportation hub?''

He didn't point out that she was interrupting again. ''Like the hub,'' he concurred. ''They can cover a story like that more effectively and more thoroughly than a wide-distribution organization. And those stories are important. They affect people's lives. But people won't be able to read them unless they turn to papers like the *Sentinel*. Circulation comes before respectability—not in lieu of. I'm sorry if I failed to communicate that to you.''

''No. I'm sorry.'' Molly's fingers quivered slightly in his. ''I should have trusted Carl to know what was best for his own paper. He wouldn't have brought you in if he'd thought you would destroy what he'd built.'' Had her expression not been so open, Sam might have thought she was teasing him. But there was nothing in her tone or the clear look of regret in her eyes to suggest that she didn't genuinely mean what she'd said. The sense of relief that flooded him also shocked him. Sam had never particularly cared what people thought of him, but for reasons he couldn't explain, Molly's opinion seemed vital.

She shook her head. ''I've made this much harder than I should have, Sam, and I'm a big enough person to admit it.''

''I appreciate that,'' he said.

''And I give you my word that I'll do whatever I can to help you.''

''There are going to be some tough changes

ahead,'' he replied, giving her a close look. "Probably some job cuts—or at least reassignments.''

"You're going to get rid of Bob Flayland, aren't you?''

Sam wasn't surprised at her insight. Molly knew the *Sentinel* as well as anyone, maybe better. Bob Flayland had been senior editor of the community news section for twenty years. He was past his prime and out of touch with the majority of the potential readership. "I'm going to suggest to Bob that he start writing a weekly op ed. It'll give him more freedom to voice his opinions, and the community knows and respects his name. It seems like a natural fit.''

"It does. It's brilliant.''

"Thanks,'' he said with a quick grin. "Hearing that from you feels a little like winning an Olympic medal.''

Molly laughed. "Oh, come on. It hasn't been that bad.''

"I've never worked harder for a compliment in my life,'' he confessed.

"For your information, I think you have lots of good ideas. I just don't happen to think the advice column and the coupon clipper are among them. Nor,'' she frowned at him slightly, "is the idea of doing away with the coverage of the duck races.''

Sam rolled his eyes. "You're never going to let up on that, are you?''

"Not until you change your mind.''

"The last time I changed my mind I was twenty years old and thinking about dropping out of college.''

"And see,'' she shot back, "it turned out that

changing your mind was the right thing to do. Where would you be today if you hadn't finished your degree?''

In spite of himself, Sam chuckled. "You win. I'll give you until Saturday to change my mind. Deal?''

"Deal.'' Apparently satisfied, Molly changed the subject. She spread her arms and looked up at the height of the mast. "How do you ever make yourself leave this?''

"It's not easy," he told her.

"*This* is where you spend your weekends," she guessed. "It has nothing to do with wanting to get out of Payne and everything to do with wanting to get back to this.''

"Usually," he agreed.

"I'm sorry I misjudged you," she said. "I'm a little ashamed of myself.''

"You had me pegged for a Boston society type, didn't you?''

"Not really. There's been a lot of speculation about your weekends." She paused. "Most everyone figured it was a woman.''

"But not you?''

She shrugged. "I don't know what I thought. I was just determined not to like you.''

That made him laugh. "At least you're honest about it.''

"I'm always honest. Even when it's brutal." Molly leaned back against the mast. "And while we're on the subject of honesty, I have a confession to make," she told him quietly, her voice a throaty purr that made Sam's gut clench.

"Oh?" He closed the distance between them with

a long step. He could feel the warmth of her body through her clothes. His fingers began to tingle with the anticipation of touching her. He wanted to bury one hand in her luxuriant sweep of hair, and use the other to press her tightly against him so he could feel her curves molding to his body. Sam fought an internal war for self-control and warned himself it was too much too soon. Molly wouldn't expect it. He couldn't begin to imagine how she'd react if he simply pulled her to him and kissed her as he'd been longing to do for most of the evening.

"Yes, I do." Molly glanced momentarily at the gleaming deck rails, then back at Sam. Her eyes looked dark in the soft light. Slowly, she reached for his right hand. As her fingers wrapped around it, Sam felt a charge of electricity spread up his arm and down his spine. Molly gently lifted his hand close to her face and rubbed her thumb across a healing scrape on his knuckles. Sam's heart rate accelerated. Molly studied the wound on his hand with keen interest. "I noticed this scrape this morning in your office." She slid her thumb across the rough surface. "I guess I had fallen victim to the gossip about you. I just assumed that you spent your weekends lazing around on the coast."

He wondered if she could feel his pulse pounding beneath her fingers. "I'm not the type to cycle the Vineyard and attend club gatherings, Molly," he said dryly. "I never have been."

"I think I knew that," she said. "It never seemed to really fit you." She paused. "You're a powerful man, Sam—" Before he could interrupt, she continued. "And I'm not talking about your business connections. I mean you, personally. You have a certain aura about you that commands attention and respect. It's really hard to picture you milling about with people who don't share your drive and your work ethic. I couldn't quite place you in that environment.''

''I'm glad to hear that.''

''You're an enigma—complex, mystifying.'' Molly frowned. ''On the one hand, I can imagine you're completely comfortable with your family's social circle, but on the other hand, I think you're the type of man who stands at the edge of the crowd and waits for the party to end so you can get back to something important.''

''Probably.''

She smiled slightly. ''I think that's why the scrape fascinated me.''

He tightened his fingers on hers. Molly gave him a sheepish look. ''In my experience, men of leisure don't have scraped knuckles.''

''It ruins the manicure,'' he said seriously.

Molly laughed. The throaty sound sent a wave of heat coursing through him. ''Precisely,'' she said. Her gaze dropped to the scrape again. ''I'm beginning to think I seriously underestimated you, Sam.''

''Oh?'' She had no idea, he thought.

''I think I was a little afraid of how I was feeling.''

He turned his hand in hers so he could press her palm to his chest. That had to be the best news he'd had in days. Strategy, he reminded himself, was key here. He was very, very good at strategy. He'd never needed it more than he did in this instance. ''How were you feeling, Molly?'' he probed gently.

Molly hesitated. He could almost sense the conflict

in her. "I was falling for you," she finally admitted. "Hard." She held his gaze a second longer, then turned her head down. "I fought it, but I was losing."

Sam swept an arm around her waist and pulled her tight against him. The crush of her softness against his hard length was even more satisfying than he'd imagined. Molly was exactly the kind of woman Sam most appreciated. A sharp mind and enough curves to fill a man's hands and feel womanly against his body. He'd never liked hard-angled women despite their fashionability. "That's a very good thing," he told her as he lowered his head. "A very, very good thing."

"I don't know about that."

"I do." He brought his face close to hers. He sensed her hesitation and realized this was one of the many things that attracted him to her. Molly didn't have the jaded edge of sophistication which characterized the women he generally met in his business and social life. She was fresh and invigorating. Being with her reminded him, in many ways, of sailing. She was as unpredictable as the wind—challenging, fresh and exhilarating. When he won a battle with her, he felt as though he'd struggled against insurmountable odds and somehow survived—and he couldn't wait to do it again.

Anticipation roared through him as he realized he was about to finally do something he'd been fantasizing about for weeks. He'd bet the feeling of kissing Molly would be absolutely intoxicating. "I've been wondering," he told her, "how much longer I was going to have to wait before I could kiss you."

Molly wound her arms around his neck and stood

up on tiptoe, as if his question had sent whatever shreds of resistance she had into oblivion. "Oh, good. I was afraid you were going to make me embarrass myself."

With a grunt of satisfied triumph, Sam lowered his head to cover Molly's lips. She was sweet and spicy, refreshing and utterly addictive. He moved his mouth against hers, drinking deeply as he explored her curves with his hands. Her sweatshirt did nothing to disguise a lush softness that made Sam crave the feel of her bare skin. Molly moaned as she pressed herself closer to him. Sam molded her hips to his as he deepened the kiss.

He kissed her until his body began to ache with a steady pulsing burn. She threaded her fingers into the hair at his nape where her fingertips tickled his skin.

"Molly," he muttered. "Molly, you're so sweet."

"Sam, I'm not—" She took a shuddering breath when he pressed his mouth to the shell of her ear. "I don't—" She swallowed when he blew a hot, moist stream of air into the sensitive hollow. "It's so—oh, Sam." He flicked his tongue over her earlobe. Molly shuddered.

"So soon? So fast?" he asked, pressing a kiss to the spot beneath her ear. "Tell me, Molly. Tell me what you're feeling."

She shivered. "Much," she answered. "It's so much." Her hands slid to his shoulders where she pushed him slightly away from her. "I didn't think—" She trailed off and dropped her head to his shoulder. "I *can't* think."

Sam understood. He'd had weeks to consider his attraction to Molly, what he wanted, and how he wanted to pursue her. Unless he missed his guess, she hadn't even realized what she was feeling until earlier today. He wrapped both arms around her and pulled her close. Slowly and thoroughly, he caressed her with his hands and his mouth. When he edged a hand inside her sweatshirt, he encountered a satin camisole. The texture, he guessed, couldn't be any smoother or softer than her skin. Through the slick fabric, he felt her stomach quiver as he stroked its softness.

Molly shivered and leaned against him. Her lips rubbed against his, kissing and probing, tasting and experimenting. Sam's libido kicked into overdrive when she toyed with the sensitive spot just behind his ears.

When Sam lightly cupped her breast, Molly gasped. Slowly, he lifted his head, but kept his hand in place. The firm weight of her resting against his palm had him fighting an internal battle for self-control. "You're beautiful," he told her. "Desirable."

"Sam—"

"It's okay," he assured her. "I'm not trying to rush you into anything. I just want you to know how much I want you."

She choked out a half laugh. "Whatever I'm feeling, it's not rushed. Ravished, maybe. Reeling. Ravenous."

"Ready?" Sam quipped.

"Don't push your luck." She gave his shoulder a slight swat. "This is a little sudden for me, I mean I knew I was having strong feelings toward you. I just didn't admit to myself what they were until this morning. And even then, I wasn't very happy about it."

Sam smiled into the near darkness. One thing he'd always admired about Molly was her ruthless honesty. ''I know.''

''You can't possibly know,'' she countered. She tipped her head back to meet his gaze. ''I went to work this morning expecting you to fire me.''

He cupped her cheek with his large hand. ''I had other plans.''

Molly searched his gaze. ''For how long?''

''Weeks,'' he confessed. ''I realized before you did that the obvious chemistry between us wasn't a bad thing.''

''My head's spinning. You must think I'm an idiot.''

''I don't,'' he assured her. He found her innocence charming, but knew she'd misunderstand if he tried to explain. The last thing he wanted to do tonight was begin a conversation that would require explaining the differences between Molly and the other women he'd known. His mood would definitely sour, and he doubted he could convince her that she wasn't coming up short in his eyes. ''It's like I told you this morning—there are many forms of passion.''

''I didn't imagine—''

Sam covered her lips with his thumb. ''I know. And it's okay. I'm not going to rush you into anything, but I'm also not going to lie to you.'' He paused. ''I want you, Molly. I want you to be my lover. I want to get to know you in every intimate way imaginable. I think you and I can have something explosive and exciting, and I'd like the chance to explore it before my work at the *Sentinel* is done. That's why I made this deal with you today.''

"What if I'm never ready to take that step?"

"Then you aren't." He paused, wondering if he'd gone too far or given her too much information. He suspected that Molly wasn't the type of woman who plunged into convenient, temporary liaisons. He couldn't live with himself if he misled her or gave her a false impression. Sam didn't put down stakes and sit still. He didn't form irrevocable ties and bonds that might hinder him from moving to the next place and the next project. In that way, he was very much like his father. Until now, he'd carefully chosen women who understood and shared that aspect of his nature. But Pamela had left him feeling inexplicably hollow and weary. He had needed something fresh. And he'd found it in Molly Flynn.

"The truth is," he told her, "I'm man enough to know that if you aren't ready, I won't find the experience of making love to you very satisfying. I want you to desire it as much as I do."

She searched his gaze. "You aren't put off by the idea that I might not ever want to—" She paused. "That I might not get to that point?"

He shook his head. "I'd be disappointed if that happened, but I'm not worried about it."

"You think I will," she guessed.

"I'm confident I can make you trust me. You've already said you're attracted to me. And I'm sure as hell attracted to you. I've wanted you for weeks, Molly. Those are the basic elements. The rest—like the timing and the semantics—will take care of itself."

"Sam—"

"This doesn't embarrass you, does it?"

"You don't understand," she told him. "I'm a very basic kind of person. I don't have the kind of life—"

"Are you trying to tell me you're not the kind of woman to get involved in a casual fling?"

"Now who's interrupting?"

"Sorry."

"Now that you mention it, yes—I'm not the type."

"I know that," he assured her. "Believe it or not, I like that about you. It might surprise you to learn that I'm not the type to indulge in casual affairs either. I may not enter relationships with long-range plans, but neither do I enter them lightly. My father took relationships lightly." He couldn't quite keep the bitter note from his voice. "It didn't turn out that well for him," Sam said flatly.

"I'm feeling a little overwhelmed."

"This has been a lot to take in in a day, hasn't it?"

Molly nodded. "I don't think I've ever had this many emotional mood swings in one day. It's got to be a record."

Sam laughed softly. "Then we're even. Since the day I walked into the *Sentinel,* I haven't been able to decide whether I wanted to strangle you or seduce you."

"I'll bet the jury's still out on that," she quipped.

"Sometimes," he admitted. "But I have to confess, I'm even beginning to enjoy arguing with you."

"Good thing. I have a feeling there's a lot of that in our future."

He dipped his head to press a soft kiss to her forehead. "Well, you know what they say about the best part of arguing."

"Making up?"

"Mm-hmm." He kissed her lightly. "Definitely."

Molly's eyes fluttered shut. "Sam—" she said.

And he decided he could get addicted to the way she said his name.

# Chapter Five

"Sam, you're never going to guess—" Molly skidded to a stop on the soft carpet just inside Sam's office when she noticed two older women seated across from his desk. One was exquisitely dressed in a designer suit with matching pumps and handbag. Elegant and sophisticated, she wore her graying brown hair pinned up in a sweep of thick, soft-looking waves. The other woman wore clothes that Molly would have sworn came from a thrift shop, had they not conveyed a certain indefinable priciness. Her long, flowing skirt had a muted batik pattern. Her cashmere sweater had a hand-dyed look that made it seem exotic, despite its relatively undramatic hue. Her hair was also long with streaks of gray, though its strawberry blond color made them less noticeable. She'd pulled it back from her face with a turquoise-encrusted headband, and she wore pearl earrings so large they should have looked artificial, but her poise and bearing defied anyone to assume they weren't genuine.

"Um, hi," Molly called to Sam. "Karen didn't tell me you had company."

Sam had risen from his desk upon Molly's precipitous entrance. He was making his way toward her with a look of both relief and warning in his eyes. Her heart accelerating at the sight of him, Molly realized her real reason for coming here this morning had nothing to do with the information in her hand.

He'd driven her home last night, her hand clasped firmly in his in the close confines of his car. Molly's pulse, still racing from the boathouse, had not yet slowed when he'd walked her to her front door and kissed her, hard, thoroughly, and with a passion that had left her breathless. The look in his eyes had been unmistakable. If she'd given him even the slightest indication that she was willing, he'd have taken her straight to bed. She'd fought an internal war with common sense versus desire and passion. It had left her feeling slightly drained when she'd finally managed to whisper, ''good night'' and close the door. Somehow she knew he'd waited there until she'd turned the key in the dead bolt. Molly had leaned against the cool wood door, listening to the sound of his footsteps retreating down her walk.

When she'd heard his car door close she knew that he'd finally left. The image of him standing outside her door, just out of reach, waiting only for her invitation, had followed her to bed where she'd tossed and turned, wondering what she'd gotten herself into.

Molly had been with men before, but never had she felt such a shaky, overwhelming feeling of passion and desire. She knew now what her sisters had been telling her for years. Molly had tumbled into relationships before, but she'd always been in charge. Until Sam, no one had toppled her off her feet, swept her into a storm of possibilities, and given her this feeling of perpetual dither. Her stomach was in knots, her pulse was too fast, her heartbeat was irregular. Even her skin seemed warmer than usual. If it's not passion, she mused, then it's the flu.

Sam was looking at her curiously. "Molly," he said quietly. "I'm glad you're here."

Her gaze darted quickly between the two women, then back to Sam. She wasn't ready to explain her relationship with him, not to her family, her friends, or to these two strangers who were watching her with keen interest. What was she supposed to tell them? That she suddenly wanted—no, *craved* him—after all these weeks of irritation and anger?

She'd been relieved to see the note she'd left herself yesterday, reminding her to talk to Sam about a discovery at the county clerk's office. It gave her a reason to see him this morning. She wouldn't have to broach the subject of whether or not he too had spent his night heated and bothered with longings. She'd headed straight to his office and been waved through the door by Karen, who was on the phone at the time.

Sam's expression was slightly amused, telling her all too clearly that he knew exactly what she was thinking. Molly had to fight a blush. The corner of his mouth twitched. "I was just going to have Karen call and see if you could come up for a minute. I have someone I wanted you to meet," he told her.

Molly shoved the note from her desk into the back pocket of her jeans. "Oh," she said, feeling awkward under the close scrutiny of the two women.

Sam placed a hand at the small of her back and

guided her forward. "Genelle, Aunt Margaret, this is Molly."

Molly immediately recognized the names. This was Sam's stepmother—Edward Reed's widowed wife—and her eccentric older sister, Margaret DeVie. "Hello," she said as the two women rose. She moved forward and extended her hand, suddenly aware of an ink stain on her index finger. "I'm Molly Flynn."

Genelle Reed's smile was more genuine than Molly had expected. Another miscalculation on her part, she thought resignedly. "It's very nice to meet you. Margaret and I were just in the process of chastising Sam for keeping you secret from us."

Sam shook his head. "It wasn't you I kept it from. It was Taylor."

"Your sister's got the wedding planned, you know," Margaret assured him. "You know how she is."

"Unfortunately," Sam concurred, but his voice held a hint of humor. "Now that Ben's married, I'm Taylor's latest project."

"At least she's taken to planning *other* people's weddings," Margaret said. "Instead of just her own."

That made Genelle laugh. "Now, Margaret, don't be so hard on Taylor. She means well."

"She's the only woman I know who has planned five weddings for herself and hasn't made it down the aisle for any of them."

Sam indicated a spare chair for Molly while he sat on the edge of his desk. "Genelle and Margaret drove down from Boston today," he told her, "because they didn't want to wait any longer to meet the woman who finally got the better of me."

Molly winced. "I hope Sam explained that the ad—"

"Oh, I understand perfectly, dear," Genelle said as she lowered herself gracefully back into her chair. "Sam is a dear boy, but I swear he can drive even a patient woman to desperation."

Molly glanced at Sam. He was watching his stepmother with easy benevolence. She didn't know how to respond, so she merely waited.

Margaret concurred with her sister. "I'm sure you don't have to tell Molly that. But at least she took him to task for it."

"Unlike Pamela," Genelle said.

Sam's expression registered a flicker of annoyance. "Genelle," he said, warning in his tone.

His stepmother took the cue. "Don't worry, dear," she assured him. "I don't want to discuss that woman any more than you do." She looked at Molly. "Tell me, Molly, how hard has it been to work for Sam these past few weeks?"

A smile played at the corner of Molly's mouth. "Next to impossible," she admitted. "He's not very flexible."

"And you are?" Sam shot back.

"I don't have to be," she told him. "I'm not the one making the decisions."

"For which we can all thank God." Sam glanced at his family. "Molly would have this paper out of business in a quarter if it were up to her."

"I would not," she countered. "I just wouldn't do away with something crucial like coverage of the duck races."

"Duck races?" Margaret and Genelle said in unison.

"Long story," Sam assured them. "I'll tell you later."

"Important story," Molly muttered.

Genelle laughed. "I see why you like her, Sam." She looked at Molly. "I'm really not here to take up your time—" she flashed a brief smile at her stepson "—or Sam's. I just came to meet you and issue you an invitation."

"Invitation?"

Genelle nodded. "I'm sure Sam hasn't told you."

"I haven't," Sam said bluntly.

"He's hoping we'll forget the entire thing," Margaret told Molly.

Molly glanced at Sam. "What thing?"

"It's ridiculous," Sam said.

"No," his stepmother insisted. "It is not."

"Taylor's been planning it for weeks." Margaret drummed her fingers on the arm of her chair.

"Taylor plans everything for weeks," Sam pointed out.

"Planning what?" Molly asked.

Genelle smoothed an invisible wrinkle from her skirt. "We're celebrating Sam's birthday next week. Taylor is hosting a party. We'd all like it if you'd come."

Curious, Molly thought. Sam had told her he had some business to take care of in Boston that weekend, but that he'd return on Saturday morning for the duck races. The birthday had not come up. His lips pressed into a thin line and she sensed a tension in him she couldn't define. "I'd love to," she replied carefully.

He gave her a probing look. "I'm not even sure I'm planning to go."

Margaret clucked her tongue. "Don't be ridiculous, Sam. You're not going to disappoint Taylor, and you know it."

"I told her not to do this."

"And she's never listened to you when you gave orders," his stepmother retorted. "Why should she start now?" She looked at Molly. "Don't let him fool you. I think he'd appreciate it if you came."

Molly watched Sam. "We'll talk it over," she said, certain of that much at least.

Genelle and Margaret rose to leave. Genelle leaned over and kissed Sam gently on the cheek. "Don't worry, dear," she told him. "Taylor promises she won't embarrass you."

He didn't respond. Margaret extended her hand to Molly. "It was very nice meeting you, young lady." She nodded toward Sam. "Hard as it might seem, try to keep him from working himself to death."

Molly nodded. "I will." She waited while Sam walked the two women to the door. He was cordial and apparently relaxed, yet she sensed an underlying tension. She'd never met a man with as many different layers as Sam Reed. He accepted his stepmother's farewell kiss, hugged his aunt, then shut the door behind the two women, pausing for several heartbeats before turning to face her.

"Well," he said. "You've had your first taste of the Reeds."

"You say that as if I just survived some initiation ritual."

"My family is a little—intense."

That made her laugh. "Geez, Sam, wait'll you meet mine."

He seemed genuinely baffled by the comment, but didn't respond, so Molly forged ahead. "Actually, I kind of have a theory about that. I think every family is weird—you just don't necessarily see it from the outside. Once you're close to 'em, though—" She smacked her hands together. "Whammo."

Sam's expression remained mercurial. "You may have a point there."

"Oh, definitely." Molly rose from her chair and crossed the plush carpet toward him. "So, um, when were you planning to tell me about the birthday party?"

"As late as I possibly could and still get away with it."

"Come on, Sam, don't tell me you're the I-can't-stand-getting-old type."

"I have nothing against getting old."

Complex, she reminded herself. Sam was incredibly, sometimes even infuriatingly, complex. She'd learned that after weeks of arguing with him in editorial meetings. Something told her she was about to reveal another of his layers. "It's just the party that makes you cranky," she said slowly, her understanding beginning to dawn. He looked every inch the powerful businessman today. Conservatively dressed in a white shirt and dark trousers, he wore a fashionable tie perfectly knotted at his throat. She glanced quickly at the still-healing scrape on his knuckles to remind herself of the man behind the facade. "And by the way, who is Pamela?" She'd detected a note in his voice when his stepmother had mentioned the woman's name, a hard note she hadn't heard since the day he'd fired the source-fabricating journalist in an editorial meeting.

"No one important," Sam said flatly.

Sure, Molly thought. "Oh, really?"

"Yes. Really."

Molly decided now was not the time to press the issue of Pamela. There'd be plenty of opportunities later. Vaguely, she remembered him saying something about a former relationship and its disastrous end during their conversation yesterday. But she'd been too preoccupied to catch its significance. She had assumed he was talking about Pamela Quorrus, the Boston socialite and blue-blooded member of the politically powerful and wealthy Quorrus clan. When Sam had arrived at his brother's wedding with Pamela Quorrus, the tabloids and gossip columns had speculated widely that another Reed marriage was in the offing, but the relationship seemed to have ended before it began. Later, she promised herself, she'd find out the details. For now, she was more interested in knowing why Sam was bristling over something as simple as a birthday party. "So if it's not the age thing," she pressed, "what's got you so worked up about the party?"

He shrugged and reached for a stack of papers on his desk. "I dislike spectacles. I told you that."

"It's just a party, Sam. Not the invasion of Normandy."

He regarded her with a raised eyebrow. "You have no idea what's entailed in one of my sister's parties. It's *never* just a party."

She shook her head. He looked determined, but so

was she. She pictured the expression on his face last night when he'd kissed her in the boathouse. It had showed a side of Sam she'd never seen before. The side that avoided telling her about this party, and for reasons other than his schedule or a slight annoyance with his sister. There was a vulnerability to that side of him that Molly was powerless to resist. "That's not good enough, Sam." Molly crossed her arms over her chest. "I want the details."

"There are no details."

"I'm not buying that. I'm a journalist. I'm naturally suspicious, intuitive and pushy."

"What if I told you it's none of your business?"

"Then we'll fight." She frowned at him. "You gave me the right to ask these questions yesterday. Consider it a VIP press pass with unlimited private and exclusive interviews."

"Molly—"

"I'm serious. You're the one who said you wanted to be involved. We're not just going to pretend, we're actually going to get to know one another. I distinctly remember—"

Sam muttered a dark curse and rounded his desk to stare out the window. She noted that in the morning sunlight, his hair looked lighter. She could see a slight reddish cast where the sun had kissed the ends of his dark waves. Molly impatiently tapped one foot while she waited in the thickening silence. Finally, he turned toward her again. "I have no idea why Taylor got this harebrained idea. I told her not to do it."

"Maybe she just wanted to do something nice for you."

"She did," he agreed. "Taylor might be eccentric,

but she's generous—sometimes to a fault.'' He raked a hand through his hair. Molly had learned he only did that when he was intensely agitated. It gave him a rumpled look she found blatantly sexy. ''I don't celebrate birthdays,'' he said simply. ''I never have.''

''If it's not about getting old, then why not?''

''Because,'' he thrust his hands into his pockets. ''I don't actually know when mine is.''

Molly took a moment to absorb that. ''You're kidding.''

He shook his head. She frowned, the thought alien to her. In the extended and immediate Flynn family, birthdays might as well be federal holidays for all the pomp and circumstance surrounding their celebration. ''You're *not* kidding,'' she said. ''Why not?''

''I don't find anything funny about it.'' His voice was curt.

She blinked. ''What? Oh, no, I mean why don't you know, not why aren't you kidding.''

''The event obviously wasn't newsworthy enough for my mother to share when Edward took me in,'' Sam shrugged. ''And he didn't ask.''

''What does it say on your driver's license?''

''October 15. It's sometime in October, or at least, that's what my mother cited in her paternity suit against Edward. She claimed they'd had a brief affair the February before I was born. Whether it was true or not, Edward didn't contest it. He picked the fifteenth of October, and I've used it officially ever since.''

''So your sister—''

''Taylor likes to plan things. She especially likes to plan weddings, but she's having a dry spell.'' He leaned back against the desk. "Frankly, I was hoping my involvement with you would distract her from the birthday party."

"You'd rather have her planning your *wedding?*"

"Any day. I can call off a wedding. I'm stuck with a birthday."

Molly nodded. "I see."

"Do you?"

"Sure. You've got it in your head that if the date of your birthday never mattered enough for your own mother to write it down, then you shouldn't bother observing it either."

"Something like that."

"That's just dumb, Sam," she said bluntly.

He frowned. "Thanks for your opinion."

"Well, sorry, but it is." Molly joined him by the desk. "I mean, where'd you get the stupid idea that birthday parties are all about you? The rest of us have a say in it, too, you know. It's kind of like, welcome to the world, Sam; glad you could join us, Sam; thanks for being a part of our lives, Sam. We celebrate birthdays because it's one of the few opportunities we have to celebrate life and family and community."

"And getting old."

"I thought you said it had nothing to do with that."

"It doesn't," he said. "I just fail to understand why people who are obsessed with age are also obsessed with birthdays. Doesn't that strike you as a contradiction?"

Molly shook her head. "It's just human nature—it's one of the things that bind us together. *Everyone* has a birthday."

"I don't," he said.

"Sure you do. Just because you don't know when it is doesn't mean you don't have one." Molly shrugged. "So tell me about this party."

"Tell me first why you came up here," he said, deftly changing the subject.

She shoved her hand in her pocket and pulled out the note she'd left herself the day before. "Yesterday at the county clerk's office," she told him, "I jotted this down, and I forgot to mention it to you last night. I thought you might want to put in a call about it." She handed him the piece of paper.

Sam scanned it, then raised an eyebrow. "Interesting."

"That's what I thought." She crossed her arms over her chest. "I still want to know about the birthday party."

He picked up his electronic organizer, flipped it open and pressed a couple of buttons. "I've got a contact in Boston that can help us with this."

"What am I supposed to wear?"

He shot her a dry look as he reached for the phone. "This might not mean anything, you know."

"Maybe not," Molly conceded. "And when is it, exactly? I have to check my schedule."

Sam punched a number into the phone. "I have no idea. I'm not planning to go." She could hear the phone ringing on the other end through his speaker phone.

"Liar," Molly shot back. "You're not going to disappoint your sister."

He raised an eyebrow as the phone continued to ring. "When did you develop such a high opinion of me? Two days ago I was smug and prone to tantrums.''

Molly fought a blush. ''I wouldn't say I have a high opinion of you—I just recognize you for what you are.''

Someone answered the other end of the line. ''Miss Bradson's office.''

Sam grabbed the receiver and held it to his ear. ''Hi, Carolyn, this is Sam Reed.'' He paused. Molly watched him as he propped the phone against his shoulder and visibly relaxed. He was back in his comfort zone. Tracking down a business lead was easy. Talking about his birthday had been driving him crazy.

She factored that observation into her emerging picture of Sam. Meeting his stepmother and aunt had provided another interesting revelation about his life. He was a little edgy about his family. Though he had taken Edward Reed's name at some point, he still stood apart from the Reed clan with an aloofness that Molly found fascinating. Though fully aware of his role as one of Edward Reed's heirs, something she couldn't quite define said he'd accepted the mantle through necessity and had never quite forgiven himself for it.

Sam finished his conversation and hung up the phone. ''You were right,'' he said, ''Cobell's contractor for the transportation hub is the same firm that was investigated last year in Atlantic City for that casino project. They changed their trade name after they filed for Chapter Eleven bankruptcy protection.''

''It doesn't necessarily mean anything.''

''No,'' he conceded, ''but it might.'' He passed her

the piece of paper with her notes from the day before. "Stay on it. See where it takes you."

Molly stuffed the note back into her pocket. "I plan to. Now, about the party."

"You aren't going to let it drop, are you?"

She shook her head. He hesitated for a moment before he slid one arm around her waist and pulled her forward until she stood between his slightly outspread legs. He was still leaning against the desk, and she could feel his corded thighs on either side of her hips. Her ears started to ring.

Molly took a shaky breath. "Sam—" This was exactly what she'd feared. The strong tug of attraction she'd felt yesterday had not ebbed with a good night's sleep. Last night's kiss in the boathouse still had her feeling unsettled.

He raised one large hand and cupped the back of her head. "I missed you last night," he said. "In my bed."

Molly's lips parted slightly as her breathing turned shallow. "Oh?"

He swept his thumb over her lower lip. "I told you I wouldn't rush you." Sam dipped his head and pressed a moist kiss to her forehead. "I'm a very patient man."

Her hands were shaking, so Molly placed them on his chest. Immediately, she realized her mistake. She could feel the strong thud of his heartbeat and the heat of his skin through his starched shirt.

Sam urged her a little closer. "Tell me how well you slept."

Molly's gaze dropped to the spot where his collar

rested against his tanned throat. "Not very well," she confessed.

He swept a hand down her spine. "I'm glad to hear that."

When she raised her eyes again, she saw the carefully banked fire in his gaze. He bent his head to bring his face close to hers. "Let me kiss you, Molly," he said softly.

The appeal was so unexpectedly quaint that Molly forgot her very reasonable objections that they were in his office where someone might enter, and that she couldn't guarantee how far a kiss might go after the effect he'd had on her last night. Her common sense told her she was way out of her league. As she'd lain on her bed last night, her skin unexpectedly warm and her lips still tingling from his kiss, she'd been unable to shake the image of the wide leather sofa in his office and the fact that she'd see him again today.

Instead, she shifted slightly, bringing her body into exquisite contact with his, and whispered, "Oh, yes, Sam."

He took his time with the kiss, beginning with a soft, leisurely exploration of her upper lip, then her lower. His hands moved up and down the planes of her back, rubbing gently, persuading her to melt against him. Molly was fairly certain she heard bells ringing and bees buzzing, but she ignored the intrusion with a soft sigh and wound her arms around Sam's neck.

Just when her knees felt they would buckle, Sam ended the kiss with a soft curse and reached for the phone. "Reed," he barked into the receiver.

Molly blinked, slightly abashed when she realized

the ringing in her ears had been the sound of Sam's phone. Sam kept one arm around her waist. He pressed the mouthpiece of the receiver against his shoulder and mouthed, "Sorry."

Molly shook her head as she extricated herself from his embrace. Pulling the note from her pocket, she waved it at him. "I'm going downtown."

Sam covered the mouthpiece with his free hand, leaned forward and gave her a quick kiss. "Great. I'll call you tonight."

"Good. I still have questions about the party."

# Chapter Six

But Sam didn't call her that night. Nor did he come to the office the following day, or the rest of the week. Molly arrived at work Wednesday morning to find a message from him on her voice mail. A family emergency had demanded his return to Boston. He'd call, he said. He'd let her know what was happening.

By Friday, she still hadn't heard from him. She knew from conversations at the *Sentinel* that Sam had remained hands-on, despite his absence. It seemed everyone else at the paper had spoken with him that week. Only Molly had been left out of his loop. She hadn't been able to decide exactly how she felt about it. She was partially annoyed, partially intrigued, and very frustrated.

Against her better judgment, Molly gave Sam more than a few of her second thoughts. In between, she was dodging questions from her family about her relationship with him, avoiding the prying eyes of her friends, neighbors, and co-workers, and researching Fred Cobell's transportation project.

She hadn't been able to shake the image of him, one hip propped against the desk, his crisp, white col-

lar smooth against a tanned throat, watching her with
eyes that held an indefinable glint as he talked about
the birthday party. She suspected he'd been seriously
disconcerted by her insistence on knowing the details
of the party. She was certain that both his sudden
departure for Boston, and his apparent avoidance of
her all week had something to do with the event.

Friday night found Molly alone at the office, still
thinking about Sam and wondering what in the world
she'd gotten into. She finished organizing some notes
and glanced at the clock. Almost time for her friend
JoAnna's weekly call. Molly had been dying to talk
to her since the previous week when she'd fired off
that god-awful personal ad about Sam. Had JoAnna
not been out of the country on assignment, Molly
would have tracked her down with the story of her
impending demise and Sam's bizarre response. But
this week, it seemed that even JoAnna was bent on
making Molly nuts.

The phone rang right on schedule. Molly snatched
up the receiver. "Jo?"

"Hey, Molly. What's kickin', Chicken?"

"Have I got a tale for you." Molly exclaimed with
a smile as she leaned back in her chair. She propped
her loafer-clad feet on the desk with a soft sigh and
began the soothing ritual of pouring her heart out.

SAM SHOT A QUICK GLANCE at the speedometer and
eased his accelerator foot a tad. Once he had cleared
Boston's thick Friday-afternoon traffic, he could set
the cruise control and quit worrying that his lingering
frustration and simmering anger would land him in
traffic court.

His sister had begged him to stay the weekend. He was exhausted and mad as hell, she'd argued, and it probably wasn't a good idea for him to be on the road—even if the trip to Payne was only a little over two hours.

Sam hadn't wanted to explain to Taylor, or to himself, why he had to get out of Boston. For the first time since he'd taken Carl's offer to bail out the *Sentinel,* he found himself craving the quiet environs of the small, peaceful community. He liked the pace. He liked the quaintness.

And he liked Molly Flynn.

A lot.

That, Sam knew, was really what had him riding the accelerator and grinding his teeth at the traffic. He'd been unable to talk to Molly all week. The Boston situation had been worse than he'd expected, and each time he'd found himself dropping into bed well after two in the morning, he'd fought the urge to call Molly.

She'd have a unique perspective on this, he thought with perhaps his first smile of the week. He imagined Molly's reaction to the hell he'd been put through. Her color would rise. Her eyes would sparkle. Her freckles would blend together as a peach-tinted flush filled her cheeks.

He'd want her. He felt a familiar twist in his gut when he thought about it. Molly, soft and natural, confident and genuine—so different and refreshing compared to the brittle women who populated his world.

Molly smelled like lemons and mown grass. He'd finally decided on the description one morning after sharing an elevator with her in the *Sentinel* building.

He was also fairly certain that whatever scent she wore, it did not advertise itself as the scent of lemons and mown grass.

But it should. Until he'd met Molly, Sam had no idea that lemons and grass could be so alluring.

More than once he'd squelched the urge to ask what her scent was. He had known women who smelled expensive, but Molly—Molly smelled intoxicating.

He glanced at the clock on his dashboard. Nearly seven. If he pressed it, he'd make it to Payne by nine. He could try calling Molly on his cell phone, but he'd promised to call her earlier this week. He hadn't, and he didn't want to explain. Not on the phone, and not while he negotiated the heavy traffic. He wanted Molly seated across—or better yet, next to him—so he could see and touch her and fall into her warmth. Tomorrow, he'd take her to the duck races. Tomorrow, he'd lose himself in the simple pleasure of her company and the gentle amusement of Payne's Duck Races Festival. He hadn't anticipated an event so keenly for longer than he could remember, and he was smart enough to know his anticipation had nothing to do with ducks and everything to do with Molly.

At this thought, Sam checked the left lane for oncoming cars and accelerated around a pickup that was moving too slowly to suit him. Every mile, he realized with satisfaction, took him farther from Boston and closer to Molly. Somehow, he didn't think that should make him feel so good, but at the moment, the thought sustained him, like a life-preserver thrown to a drowning man.

AT EIGHT FORTY-FIVE that evening, Molly let herself into her townhouse with a weary sigh. The warmth of the old place soothed her, as usual. Despite her parents' concerns about upkeep and maintenance, Molly had fallen in love with the hundred-year-old building and its charming oddities. Once providing elegant homes for members of Payne's upper crust, the row of townhouses had fallen into disrepair during the 1950s. A grant-funded reclamation project had renovated the buildings and surrounding area, and though the contractor had managed to make them safe and livable, they maintained their authentic charm.

The floors creaked. The plaster sagged and flaked from the ceilings. The pipes groaned. The winter wind whistled in the windows.

And Molly was fairly certain there was a ghost or two in the attic. Her father swore the noises coming from beneath the roof were squirrels, but Molly had tried two different exterminators who found no evidence of squirrels—or anything else.

So Molly gladly settled on the explanation that she had a couple of friendly ghosts—remnants of an earlier age. She'd take ghosts over rodents any day.

Now she caught her reflection in the hall mirror and grimaced. The stress and long hours of the week had taken a toll. She looked worse than she had on Monday when she'd gone to work expecting to lose her job.

Getting fired, she thought with a grimace, would probably have been easier than adding the complication of Sam Reed to her life.

Molly scooped up a pile of mail her postman had slipped through the slot and thumbed through it. Two catalogs, a postcard from her cousin, Sadie, who was on a college trip to Europe, and an announcement that she'd won a million dollars—for the third time this year. As she dropped most of her mail into the antique potato bin she used for a trash can, she felt a warm rubbing sensation at the back of her legs. Molly stooped to scratch her large, chocolate-brown cat between the ears and apologized for neglecting him that week. "Sorry, Errol," she told the purring ball of silken fur. "It wasn't intentional."

Errol seemed unconcerned. By now, Molly figured, he was not only used to the long hours he spent alone in her quiet little row house, but he had grown to like them. He'd adopted Molly after trying out several other houses on the street. She'd attempted to give him away five or six times, but Errol had always returned with a slightly chastising look in his wide, blue eyes. Finally, Molly had given up trying to get rid of the large, tailless cat, and had taken him in.

In many ways, he was the perfect housemate. He never complained about her hours or her cooking. He cleaned himself meticulously. He kept the rodents out. And he was always glad to see her. She'd had boyfriends with less to recommend them.

She dropped the remaining mail on the hall table and gathered up the large animal. Purring loudly, he arched his back against her throat. "I didn't do it on purpose," she assured him. "I was just really busy."

Errol seemed to understand. Errol, God love him, always seemed to understand.

Weary from her long week and several sleepless nights, Molly made her way to the kitchen. A peanut butter sandwich and glass of milk were decidedly tempting. After her conversation with JoAnna, she'd stayed at the office another couple of hours. She'd told herself she wanted to work on the transportation story, but her eyes had strayed continuously to the phone where the red message light still blinked, indicating the saved message from Sam on her voice mail. He still hadn't called. Irritated with herself for waiting, Molly had finally stuffed her belongings in her bag and headed home.

She could work on the story here just as easily as she could at the office. And maybe, if she pulled on a pair of ratty pajamas and her bunny slippers, she wouldn't be so distracted by thoughts of Sam Reed and his strange behavior.

Errol followed her into the kitchen. Feeling guilty for leaving him alone so long that week, Molly pulled a carton of cream from the refrigerator and poured a cupful into his bowl. Errol gave her an adoring look as she set the bowl on the floor.

Errol lapped his cream, pausing occasionally to twine affectionately around Molly's legs while she made a sandwich. She filled the cat in on her discoveries about the mayor's transportation plans. Errol listened attentively, purred on cue, and waited while she finished eating. If only men were that simple.

She straightened the kitchen and climbed the stairs. She could almost hear her favorite pair of flannel pajamas calling her. Hot pink with a hearts-and-lips pattern. She'd pulled them fresh from the dryer last night. Her nieces had given them to her for Christmas last year, knowing Molly's penchant for loud and cozy pajamas.

As she descended the stairs wearing them five

minutes later, Molly wondered why no one had ever studied the therapeutic effects of fuzzy pajamas and comfortable slippers. The big, pink bunny slippers flopped on her feet in a merry rhythm, while the soft, worn flannel brushed her skin like a treasured old blanket.

She had just made herself a cup of tea and settled on the sofa to watch a late movie when her doorbell rang. Errol gave her an expectant look, and Molly glanced at the clock. It had to be her landlady. Nobody but Mrs. Pickernut would ring her bell this late without calling. The older woman had probably read something in the paper she didn't approve of, and as was her habit, walked next door to bend Molly's ear about it. Mrs. Pickernut lived alone, and Molly had figured out years ago that the woman's frequent visits to complain about the *Sentinel* merely showed a need for companionship. Mrs. Pickernut routinely watched through the curtains to see when Molly's battered orange Beetle returned to the curb in front of her townhouse.

Molly looked at Errol. "All right," she told the cat. "I'll open the door, you create the distraction. Maybe this won't take long." She pulled open the door to find an exhausted and rumpled-looking Sam Reed on her welcome mat.

"Sam?"

"May I come in?" he asked wearily.

Molly was acutely aware of her hot-pink pajamas and obnoxiously oversized bunny slippers. "Um—"

"I'm beat," he said unnecessarily. He certainly looked it. His shirt was wrinkled and damp, unbuttoned at the collar and rolled back at the cuffs. His silk tie hung loose around his neck, and his face had an angular look, suggesting he hadn't slept well in days.

Molly stepped away from the door with a slight frown. ''Sure.''

He eased into her house, pushing the door shut behind him. He leaned back against it with a soft sigh, like a man who'd made an arduous journey through untold terrors before finally reaching the safety of home. ''I should've called,'' he said quietly.

''You look like hell.''

He rolled his head to one side and gave her a quizzical grin that knocked some of the edge off her worry. He was still capable, clearly, of teasing her. ''Really?'' he said, his mouth kicking up at the corner. ''You look kind of cute.''

Molly scowled at him. ''I wasn't expecting company,''

''Lips and hearts, Molly?'' He examined the pajamas. Molly had a strong feeling he was looking at more than just her pajamas. Despite the baggy fit, she had to fight the urge to cross her arms over her chest. When Sam met her gaze again, his eyes held a banked fire. ''I didn't think that was your style.''

''I happen to like these pajamas,'' she said, refusing to apologize even though she was acutely aware that the flannel had worn thin in several revealing spots. ''They were a gift from two of my nieces.''

''I can see why you're taken with them.'' His gaze dropped to her feet. ''They match your slippers.''

Molly frowned. ''Shut up, Sam.'' She started toward the living room. He paused a moment before following her.

"I'm sorry I didn't call," he said quietly. "It's been a very long week."

She brushed a cotton throw aside in the overstuffed armchair so he could sit. Sam seemed to drop into the chair. He slipped off his loafers and lifted his sock-clad feet to the ottoman with a weary groan. "I just wanted to see you tonight." He glanced around the room. "I hope I'm not intruding."

The truth was, Molly thought wryly, Sam had intruded on her every evening and most days that week. "It's fine." She stared at him for a minute. "You really look exhausted. Are you sure you're all right?"

"Weary. Not necessarily exhausted."

Molly decided not to point out that the dark circles under his eyes and the two-days' beard growth told another story. "You want something to drink?"

"Do you have any food? I didn't stop to eat."

"Peanut butter," she answered. "I don't keep a lot on hand."

He dropped his head back against the chair. "Have you eaten already?"

"Yes."

"Thank God," he said. "I was afraid I'd have to be polite and ask if you wanted to go out."

That made Molly laugh. "In case you haven't noticed, Sam, Payne isn't exactly the kind of place where I'd go out to dinner dressed in my pajamas."

"Then give me a second to summon the energy, and I'll go make myself a peanut butter sandwich."

Molly studied the corners of his eyes where the grooves seemed to have deepened since Tuesday. She made a quick decision. "I'll get it," she volunteered, picking up her empty teacup. "I was due for a refill on my tea, anyway."

MOLLY RETURNED from the kitchen to find Sam asleep in the chair. His face, though relaxed, looked haggard. What in the world had he been doing for the last week that had sucked the life out of him? This was more than a mere dispute with his sister about a birthday party. Sam was in serious emotional pain—whether he'd admit it or not.

Her eyes dropped to his hands where the scrape across his knuckles had begun to heal. It reminded her of seeing his boat Monday night, a part of Sam's life that had simultaneously endeared him to her, yet made her recognize that their worlds were far apart. People she knew in Payne sometimes worked on their cars to avoid mechanics' fees. Sam was working on a vintage sailboat merely to restore it, with every intention of taking it out to sea.

While Molly didn't doubt that Sam had enjoyed his share of casual relationships without messy entanglements and long-term commitments, Molly wasn't as resilient. She had kept every ticket stub from every movie she'd ever seen. In fact, she collected friends, relatives, and memorabilia with the fervor of a librarian collecting books. She invested herself fully in friendships and romances. Separations were hard for her, and the decision to become involved in a person's life took more than a morning's negotiation and a swift business decision about mutual gain.

Molly put his sandwich down on the coffee table and prodded his shoulder. "Sam?"

He didn't budge. "Sam," she said more insistently.

He stirred, rolled his head to the other side of the overstuffed chair, and sank even more deeply into the seat. She'd have to blast him out of the chair with dynamite if she expected him to leave tonight.

He mumbled something under his breath. There was an indefinable tone in the sound, in the slight shift of his expression, that wrapped itself around her heart and squeezed it tightly. A lock of hair had tumbled over his forehead. Molly reached out to brush it into place. He muttered again.

She couldn't explain it, but she was sure she heard loneliness in the low sound. With a sigh of resignation, Molly reached for a cotton throw and spread it over his legs.

At least Mrs. Pickernut would have something to gossip about when she noticed Sam's sports car parked in front of Molly's house all night.

DISORIENTED, SAM TRIED to figure out where he was. Except for a slight green light which threw strange shadows around the room, it was dark. There was a warm, purring weight in his lap which a stroke of his hand confirmed was a cat.

Molly, Sam remembered. He'd returned to Payne and come to Molly. His stomach tightened into a fist of hunger. Sam realized why he'd awakened. Molly had gone to make him a sandwich. He'd evidently fallen asleep in the chair before he could eat it.

When he moved his legs, he felt a stiffness in his muscles and joints from the awkward angle of the ottoman. The cat stretched lazily awake. It purred loudly as it arched its back and rubbed its ears against Sam's legs. Sam scrubbed a hand over his face, trying to chase away the lingering fog of weariness that still held him in a tight grip. His two-day beard scraped his palm.

God, he thought, he must look like a wreck. Molly had told him so when he'd turned up on her doorstep. His eyes were beginning to adjust to the light, and Sam could make out the shadows of the furniture in Molly's living room. The green glow, he realized was coming from a night-light plugged into a hall receptacle. He pushed the illumination button on his watch to check the time.

Three-thirty. Molly must have gone to bed and left him sleeping in the chair. He tried to decide why that irritated him. Surely he hadn't expected her to take him to her bed—not tonight, and not after he'd failed to call her for a week. He doubted that she could have wakened him if she'd tried. He hadn't had more than four hours of sleep a night since he'd left town, and he was too damned old to keep those hours.

Not to mention that Molly probably wasn't amused that he'd ignored her all week. Hell, he was lucky she'd let him through the front door.

*Smooth move, Sam,* he thought wryly. How many times had his sister joked that the reason Sam remained eligible was that no woman could put up with him? His behavior tonight, no doubt, was exactly what Taylor was talking about.

As his eyes continued to adjust, he caught a glimpse of something on the coffee table. Further inspection revealed a sandwich and a glass of milk. He'd had gourmet meals that didn't look as good. He shoved the cat off his lap, ignoring its outraged cry, and reached for the sandwich.

If he were half the gentleman his stepmother had raised him to be, he'd slip quietly out of Molly's house and leave her in peace. A bouquet of flowers and an eloquently worded note of apology would follow. His sister, on the other hand, would say that diamonds got you further than flowers. Sam had a feeling that Molly wasn't going to fall for anything clichéd—no matter what the price tag. And, much to his stepmother's dismay, Sam had not always taken her advice.

He polished off the sandwich, washed it down with the milk, and reached for the cotton blanket as he moved to Molly's sofa. No way in hell was he leaving now that he'd finally gotten inside Molly's life. In the morning, he'd read her mood and determine what to do. In his experience, gifts and apology notes were for cowards.

Sam had been called many things in his life, but nobody ever mistook him for a coward.

MOLLY'S NOSE TWITCHED as she caught the scent of frying bacon. She stretched luxuriously in her four-poster bed and tried to sleep again, but the aroma made her stomach growl. She frowned and cracked her eyes open. The clock read seven-thirty. Other aromas had begun to mingle with the bacon, including the addictive scent of freshly brewed coffee.

With a soft exclamation, Molly sat upright in the bed. Sam! Sam, with his unexpected visit, was cooking breakfast and making coffee in her kitchen. After she'd covered him with the cotton blanket last night, Molly had worked for several hours, going through the volumes of notes and documents she'd collected that week.

In the back corner of her mind, she'd expected him to awaken, but Sam had slept peacefully on, and by the time she'd grown too tired to concentrate, she didn't have the heart, or the energy, to prod him out of his chair. So she'd left him sleeping and plodded up the stairs to bed. If he awoke in the night, he could find his own way out.

Evidently, he'd stayed.

And he was making breakfast.

The realization made Molly frown. Unless he'd made a trip to the store that morning, he was working miracles with a tub of peanut butter, a block of cheese, and a jar of pickles.

Molly tossed the covers aside, slid her feet into her slippers and headed for the door. She caught a glimpse of herself in the mirror, frowning at her tumble of unruly red hair. She pulled a brush through it, then abandoned the effort. Experience had taught her that the only cure for her morning hair was a shower and half a tube of mousse.

''Great,'' Molly muttered. She had super-sexy Sam cooking in her kitchen and she looked as though she'd spent the night outside in a tornado. Molly groaned and turned away. Maybe this was exactly what she needed to cure the tug on her heartstrings that she felt every time she looked at Sam Reed.

She found him in the kitchen, deftly flipping pancakes. He still wore his dark dress trousers, but he'd shed the rumpled white shirt and tie from the night before. A white T-shirt stretched taut across a sculpted chest, and broad shoulders tapered to a lean waist and trim hips.

She was suddenly starkly aware of her rumpled pajamas. Sam's dark hair lay in attractive disarray around his angular face. Molly closed her eyes for a moment. She should have known that Sam was a man who wouldn't have bad hair days. He was in control of his universe. Even his hair wouldn't dare to displease him.

He seemed to sense her scrutiny, tossing her a look over his shoulder and giving her a dazzling smile. His slight growth of beard made her groan. He looked rugged and sophisticated, handsome and decadent, and way too good in her space. "Good morning," he said brightly.

And he was a morning person. She added that to the list of his flaws she was trying desperately to maintain. "Hi."

He indicated the pan with a nod of his head. "Hope you're hungry."

"Where did you get the stuff for pancakes?" she pressed, her eyes darting to the pot of fresh coffee. "And the bacon." As she headed for the coffee, Sam seemed to anticipate her. He took a mug from her rack and slid it across the counter. "Your neighbor was up," he told her. "I begged."

Molly filled her mug. "My neighbor?" She took a sip of the dark brew as Sam turned his attention back to the pancakes. Molly's stomach growled loudly.

"The older lady." Sam tossed a pancake in the air and caught it with a deft flip of his wrist. "Next door."

Molly choked. "Mrs. Pickernut?"

"Uh, Dorothy, she said."

Molly had lived in the row house for five years and had never once heard her landlady use her first name. "You borrowed food from Mrs. Pickernut?"

"She was sitting on her porch reading the paper," Sam explained. He slid two perfectly brown pancakes onto a plate, making Molly inexplicably cranky. The last time she'd made pancakes, they'd been scorched on the outside and raw in the middle. "How many of these do you want?"

Molly ignored his question. "What she was doing," she informed him, "was watching your car to see whose house you were visiting."

Sam shrugged. "Maybe. She seemed pleased to meet me."

"Did you tell her you're the guy who took over the *Sentinel?*"

"She likes the coupon section," Sam told her with a wink.

"She would," Molly drawled. She watched him slide two more pancakes on a plate. "I hope you don't expect me to eat all that."

He added two pieces of bacon, then passed her the plate. "Breakfast is the most important meal of the day," he told her. "Or haven't you heard?"

"I've heard. And I usually try to eat it around twelve." She accepted the plate and moved to the table.

"But we've got duck races to attend," he countered.

"I know. I keep trying to tell the festival committee that if they want to do something really creative, they should start them at noon."

"I take it you aren't a morning person." He finished filling his own plate.

"You aren't the only reason I'm in a bad mood at editorial meetings," she assured him. "When you moved them to eight-thirty you pretty much guaranteed I'd be crabby."

Molly waited while Sam poured himself a cup of coffee and joined her at the table. He gave her a lopsided smile that made her stomach flip. "I'll try to remember that."

"But you won't consider changing meeting times."

"No," He picked up his fork. "I just won't take it personally when you give me lip."

"You're hilarious, Sam."

His expression turned unexpectedly serious. "I'm also sorry. I didn't mean to fall asleep last night."

"You looked exhausted," she said quietly.

"You could say that. It's been a long week."

Molly waited, but he didn't elaborate. Frustrated, she plunked her fork down on the table. "You're really annoying, you know that?"

He raised his eyebrows. "Excuse me?"

"You're annoying." She waved in his direction. "You disappeared on Tuesday with little or no explanation, and I haven't heard from you since. Then you show up at my house looking like something the cat dragged in." As if on cue, Errol, who'd been circling her feet hoping for breakfast crumbs, jumped into her lap. Molly stroked the cat's dark fur. "You make me breakfast—*breakfast,* for God's sake, and then you think you can just mention that you've been a little busy this week and that's it." She glared at him. "You have no intention of telling me where you were, do you?"

"No."

"Then you've got a lot to learn about relationships, Sam."

"No doubt."

"You don't just drop off the face of the earth without an explanation—especially after what happened between us on Monday night. That's not how it works."

"I never claimed to be good at this," he reminded her.

Irritated, Molly blew a stray curl off her forehead. "I want to know where you were."

He leaned back in his chair. "It's not worth the effort it would take to explain."

Molly was beginning to wonder what the hell she'd been thinking when she'd decided this week that she simply needed to manage him better.

She couldn't even manage her checkbook most months, much less a man like Sam Reed. She could not have chosen a more unlikely man to fall for if she'd tried. She loved her small-town existence, thrived on family gatherings and town events. Molly liked the quiet peace of Payne and its easy pace of life. Sam, on the other hand, clearly found her world—where neighbors knew her business and friends helped to bear her burdens—a foreign thing.

But Molly couldn't make herself drop the subject. And the slightly wistful look on his face reminded her of when he'd talked about his first paper route. He *wanted* her to probe. He wanted someone to rely on. Sam was desperate for the unconditional love

Molly had learned to take for granted. Despite his family's financial resources, Molly had grown up so much wealthier. She'd had the love and support of family, while Sam had struggled to define his place in Edward Reed's life.

In many ways, Sam reminded her of a stray cat she'd once begged her parents to take in. The cat had turned up on their doorstep, grateful for Molly's offering of milk and tuna fish. A thorn was deeply embedded in one paw, and Molly managed to coax the animal into letting her remove it, but not into staying through the night inside the house. The animal's persistent whining had forced Molly's parents to insist that she put the cat in a box on the porch. By morning, the cat had disappeared. Night after night, it came back, ate its meal, then disappeared into the shadows. Molly tried to befriend the animal, but it never warmed up to her. One day, the cat had not returned for its meal, and Molly never saw it again.

Sam, she sensed, was much like that cat. He would accept what she gave, but something in his psyche kept him from giving back. He was guarded and careful, protective of his privacy and extremely independent. In another era, he might have pursued the life of a gunslinger. He would come into town, do a job he thought needed doing, and move on before he could form attachments.

As a child, Molly had been hurt by the cat's desertion. As an adult, she'd found over and over again that she was incapable of turning away wounded strays, despite the danger of betrayal.

The secret, she knew, was to accept the very real possibility of a broken heart as the price for taking in a stray. But somehow, the stakes seemed higher with Sam.

Studying the mercurial look in his eyes, she wondered how she could ever compare him to anything as harmless as a stray cat. A stray mountain lion, maybe—with the wits, speed, and power to match. He was trouble, her mind told her—but the wary look in his eyes made her heart race.

In her entire life, Molly had never been able to turn her back on that *please-teach-me-to-trust-you* look.

She exhaled a slow sigh. "All right, Sam, I think we need to get a few things straight here."

He gave her that wary look again, then cast a quick glance at her kitchen clock. "What time are the races?"

"We've got time," she assured him. "I've done some thinking this week—about us."

He shifted in his chair and picked up the lopsided clay napkin holder one of her nieces had given her for Christmas last year. "Really?" he said, examining the object.

"Yes." Drawing a steadying breath, Molly told herself to get a grip. The quivers and quakes his presence set off in her nervous system, she supposed, was what the poets meant by elemental attraction. There was something about Sam Reed that reminded her of the earth—powerful, unpredictable, rock solid. "And since we have a few minutes," she told him, "I'd appreciate it if we could work some things out."

He set the napkin holder down. "What kind of things?"

"Things about being involved, and what that means. I think we have different definitions."

"Ah." His tone was noncommittal.

Molly waited, but Sam didn't elaborate. Patience, she could hear Sister Mary Claire explaining, was a godly virtue. "I was wondering exactly what you think is entailed in getting involved with me," she pressed. "I mean, besides the sex part. Which I have to say you were making a fairly obvious priority before Tuesday."

His dark eyebrows drew down, and she practically heard the gears in his head turning. "Is this going to be a gender thing?"

Sister Mary Claire with her lectures on patience and long suffering, had never encountered a man like Sam. "A gender thing?"

"I've found that when women ask questions I don't understand—particularly when they already seem to know the answers to those questions—it's usually because the typical male response—that would be mine—isn't going to live up to the typical female expectation—that would be yours. So before I get myself into a hell of a lot of trouble, I figured I'd just ask. That way I'll find out what you want me to say and save us both a lot of grief."

The blunt answer completely defused her irritation. He looked so impossibly serious, Molly laughed out loud. "Geez, Sam, are you this blunt when you negotiate media mergers?"

"Media mergers are a piece of cake compared to this. Does this mean we're changing the subject?"

"Not a chance."

He took a long sip of his coffee as if seeking fortification. He set his mug on the table with careful precision. "Look, Molly, before we start this, I think you need to know that I'm not any good at it."

"Good at what?"

"Personal conversations."

"You do plenty well at arguing with me," she said. "You've been doing it for six weeks."

"That's arguing. It's different."

"Why?"

"Arguing is direct and to the point. This requires patience, and I don't have it. The last woman I dated almost went berserk trying to get me to talk about my feelings. I *do* things, I don't talk about them."

"I see."

His gaze narrowed. "That sounds suspicious."

"No. Not really. I'm just trying to figure you out."

"What's to figure?"

"You keep surprising me, Sam."

"Is that a good thing or a bad thing?"

"I'm not sure," she confessed. "Jury's still out on that."

"And in the interim?"

"I think we need to agree on some rules."

He looked a little apprehensive. "Rules?"

"Yes, rules. Since you've been gone, I've had some time to think over what you said on Monday, and I get the feeling that you expect to have a pretty big influence in my life for the next few weeks." Lord, she thought, did she sound as much like a prude as she thought? How did he manage to do this to her?

"You could say that."

"When you said that we weren't merely going to pretend to be involved—" she hesitated. "I have to tell you, I thought you meant a little more than convenient sex.''

''We haven't had convenient sex. We haven't even had inconvenient sex.''

''We would have on Monday night if I'd been willing.''

''Granted.''

''And then Tuesday, you left town and I haven't heard from you since. Sorry, Sam, that's not what I think of when I picture a mutually satisfying relationship.''

He had the grace to wince. ''I was trying to get everything done so I could get back here for today.''

''You had time to call everyone else on staff,'' she pointed out. ''I'm not pouting, Sam, I'm just a little confused. I need to know what the ground rules are.''

He nodded thoughtfully. ''Fair enough. I've handled this badly.''

Her eyebrows rose. ''I wouldn't say—''

He shook his head, stopping her objection. ''No. It's true. Hell, my sister's been on my case all week about it.''

''You've been with your sister?''

''I'll get to that in a minute.'' He drew a weary breath. ''I've wanted you a long time, Molly. I told you that on Monday. I was glad to find out the attraction is mutual.''

''I think it was the day I called you an arrogant pigheaded jerk that tipped you off.''

The corner of his mouth tilted into a smile. ''No. It was the way you looked at my legs after you said it.''

''I hate to break this to you, Sam, but I've never

even noticed your legs.'' She idly rubbed at a dent in the wood table with the pad of her thumb. ''But that doesn't necessarily mean anything,'' she continued. ''I'm not like you, Sam.''

''How do you mean?''

''Any one of my sisters will tell you, I might fall fast and hard into relationships, but I take them seriously.''

''And you think I'm not serious?''

''I think that I would never use a relationship to further my agenda in this town.''

''Is that the impression I gave you?''

She nodded. ''Isn't that your plan?''

''Actually,'' he said, ''you might be surprised to learn that my only concern here is for Carl and the future of the *Sentinel*. If the people in Payne don't particularly like me—'' he shrugged his broad shoulders ''—I'm not sure I care.''

''I didn't mean that the way it sounded.''

''Then what do you mean?'' he asked. ''You've never had trouble telling me what you think.''

But her heart had never been involved, either. ''All I'm saying is that we're going to have to face a lot of people today. I thought—after Monday, I thought…'' Her words trailed off.

Sam watched her with narrowed eyes. ''Go on,'' he prompted.

She plunged in. ''I didn't think it would bother me to stand up in front of this town and say, 'here's Sam, and I'm with him.'''

''But now it does?''

''When you feel like it's okay to leave town for a

week and not even tell me where you are, I feel like I'm lying to people I really care about.''

''Because they're going to think we have a relationship that's different from the one you think we have?'' he guessed.

She nodded. ''Obviously, you're the kind of man who can tolerate a casual relationship.'' She paused. ''And I'm not the kind of woman who even *has* casual relationships.''

Sam seemed to consider that. ''I didn't think you were,'' he said finally.

She found courage in that and forged ahead. ''And that's why I think we need some rules.''

''So you said.''

''I won't be able to stand it if I don't know when you're pretending and when you're not. It'll drive me crazy.''

''And to avoid that, you want rules.''

''Yes.'' She was beginning to warm to the topic. Sam hadn't laughed at her, nor had he refused to take her seriously. Molly thought this was a very good sign.

Sam steepled his fingers beneath his chin and regarded her with a steady look. ''So were you thinking about who pays for dates and who drives when we're going somewhere together?''

She frowned. Maybe this *wasn't* going as well as she'd hoped. ''No.''

''And I'm guessing you like the toilet paper to roll off the top?'' he continued. ''That's okay. I can live with that.''

Wearily, she looked at him. ''No.''

"No? Really? I had you pegged for an over-the-topper."

"Sam—"

"But off the bottom's fine with me, though I confess I don't usually pay much attention. I'll try to remember."

Molly's hands tightened on the edge of the table. "Will you please shut up?"

He threw her an irreverent grin. "Sorry. Sometimes I can't resist the urge to goad you."

"I've noticed that." She frowned at him. "And I'm sorry if this seems ridiculous to you. I just haven't mastered your level of disdain for other people's feelings."

That sobered him. "I'm not making fun of you," he assured her.

"You could have fooled me."

"Hell, Molly, I told you I'd screw this up. I'm tired and I've had a rough week."

She reached for her patience. "Will you just hear me out, please?"

"Yes," he agreed readily. "I'm listening."

"All I'm trying to say is that I don't want to feel like I'm lying to people. I think it'll be best for both of us if you realize that just because I've agreed to spend time with you—no matter what the reasons— it doesn't mean that I'm giving you any personal liberties. I've decided that wouldn't be wise."

"No personal liberties. Got it."

"Thank you for understanding."

He waited several long seconds. "Are you going to explain what that means?"

Molly frowned. "You know what I mean."

"Would this be a bad time for me to say that I have no idea what you're talking about?"

"You're going to make me say this, aren't you?"

"I hate to break it to you, but I'm sort of in the dark here. If you've got some invisible line you don't want me to cross, you'd better spell it out."

Her patience ran out. "I don't want you to think that just because you're going to be with me a lot, that you have any rights to me."

He stilled immediately. As if entering the eye of a hurricane, she felt an ominous calm settle in the room.

"Molly." He leaned forward so his face was level with hers. "Are you trying to tell me that you don't want to have a physical relationship with me?"

She fought the urge to squirm. "Yes."

"There's something between us, Molly. I thought I showed you that on Monday."

"You did."

"And you think you can fight it."

"I think it would be wise. Obviously, you're not planning to stay in Payne for long. If we get physically involved—"

"How do you know what I'm planning to do?" he challenged.

"Your life is somewhere else. Mine is here. Whatever's between us is temporary."

"And you're not willing to explore the possibilities, are you?" He frowned at her. "What if I tell you that I don't think we're going to be able to resist? I think there's a fire waiting to ignite. All it needs is one spark to start a conflagration."

"I think that if we both take steps to prevent it, we'll be fine. We're reasonable adults. I've admitted that I find you attractive. You've said you find me attractive. It's inevitable that our proximity will have some effect."

"*Some* effect?"

She couldn't decide if he sounded irritated or amused. "All I'm saying is that I don't see any reason at all why we can't simply agree to be friends and not let this situation go to our heads."

He studied her with a disarming stare. Usually, his mind traveled so fast, she found it difficult to follow his train of thought. Occasionally, however, he'd latch on to something with an intensity that practically took her breath away. "And you think that if I agree not to touch you, that whatever is going on between us will go away? Is that it?"

Relieved, she nodded. "Yes."

He pursed his lips in thought, then shifted to lever himself out of his chair. Placing one hand on either arm of the chair, he leaned forward so his face was level with hers. His breath fanned warm against her cheek. "Sam—"

"It won't work," he told her softly.

"I think—"

"It won't work," he told her again.

"Sam—"

"You want to know why?"

Not really, Molly thought grimly. She already knew why. She already knew that Sam made her pulse beat faster. She already knew that she felt shivers up and down her spine when he spoke in that certain tone. "I know why," she admitted.

Sam's lips slanted into that devil-take-it grin. "Good." He tipped his head closer.

"Crud," Molly muttered. "This is a bad idea," she told him.

He leaned forward so his lips were a fraction of an inch from hers. "Bet I can get you to change your mind about that," he whispered.

"No—"

"Sure I can." Sam wet his lips with the tip of his tongue. "Watch me." He closed the final distance and covered her mouth with his.

The kiss was simultaneously gentle and demanding, soft and seductive. Sam's lips glided over hers, and Molly felt herself melting into the overstuffed chair. She moaned slightly when his tongue traced the crease of her lips. Sam lifted one hand and gently touched the curve of her throat. She gasped in surprise. He took full advantage and swept his tongue inside her open mouth.

She felt warm and weightless, dizzy and desirable, as if she were floating on a warm cloud of sensation. Molly slipped one hand around his neck to touch the warm skin of his nape.

With a soft groan, Sam raised his head. "Molly, you want to explain to me how I'm supposed to keep from touching you?"

"I just don't want us to get into a situation where either of us is confused about what's going on. Where we don't know the line between truth and fiction."

Sam appeared to consider that. "I'll tell you what, Molly. I'll make you a deal."

"A deal?"

"Yep. I'll agree not to touch you again until you ask me."

She searched his gaze again, but found no hint of guile. He looked utterly sincere. "What makes you think I'll ask?"

"Because I know you feel the same electricity I do when we're together. You just haven't surrendered to it yet, as I have. When you do, you won't be able to resist."

"What do I have to agree to?"

"Not to ask unless you're absolutely sure you're ready for me. I won't wait for a second invitation."

Molly had the feeling this was a losing bet, but at the moment, it seemed like a lifeline. Temporary, she reminded herself. Sam's stay in Payne was temporary. She didn't have to resist him for long—just until he left. Then her life could get back to normal. And lonely, a quiet voice insisted in her head. Molly dismissed the voice and clenched her hands on both arms of the chair. She could do this. She *had* to do this.

Her honor demanded that she keep her bargain with Sam and prevent him from any further embarrassment about the personal ad. He'd just offered her a way to do that and still keep her heart intact. Molly nodded slowly. "All right. It's a deal."

Sam's grin was suspiciously triumphant. "Great." He moved away from her chair. "Now, if you don't mind, I'd like to grab my bag out of the car and take a quick shower. I'll clean up and we can leave from here."

That's just what she needed, she thought grimly. She had enough trouble keeping her mind off Sam without picturing him in her shower. "Um, sure."

"Great." He winked at her. "I'm in a hurry to see the ducks."

## Chapter Seven

"Go!" Molly leaned over the side of the fence and encouraged the scraggly duck she'd chosen from the pen. "You can do it," she called. "Dig, dig, dig, dig, dig."

Sam shot her an amused look and took a sip of his coffee. The brisk October air had tinted her cheeks red, and the breeze played havoc with her hair. She wore faded jeans and a Stamford University sweatshirt. Her thick hair, clasped in a loose ponytail at the nape, made his fingers itch to free it. In bed in his Boston apartment he'd found himself wondering how Molly would look sprawled against dark sheets, her hair mussed and spread across his pillows.

Molly, he was learning, did everything with reckless abandon. If he'd doubted it, the harrowing ride to the fair grounds that morning had confirmed it.

Molly had wanted to drive. Sam decided it would give him a chance to listen to her car on the road and see if he could identify the source and cause of the orange Beetle's horrific exhaust leak. As soon as she coasted through the first stop sign, he recognized his mistake. Molly drove with the same recklessness she used to argue with him in editorial meetings. As far as he could tell, there was a logic to it somewhere, but it defied description and kept him on the edge of his seat.

He'd forced himself not to cringe as she darted between cars and sneaked through yellow lights. Payne had only four traffic lights, and its citizens, he'd observed, went to extraordinary lengths to avoid them.

Now, he knew why.

Word had to be out that, at any moment, Molly might come storming through an intersection in her dilapidated car. Fortunately they could always see her coming—or at least smell the exhaust. Tomorrow, he promised himself, he would insist that he look at her car.

*If I live that long,* he thought with a grimace as her tires squealed around another curve. To take his mind off the certainty of impending collision, he concentrated on the way her long fingers gripped the steering wheel, and how the smooth curves of her face were partially shielded by her dark sunglasses. Then he asked her about new developments in her research into Cobell's transportation project. She talked while she drove, darting, as usual, from one idea to the next. He enjoyed the vibrant thrum of her voice.

Occasionally, a hint of an Irish accent would cradle a word with a rolled *r. Like a purr.* He wondered if he could get her to purr like that by whispering something forbidden in her ear.

He reveled in watching her now as she cheered and encouraged the ducks. Monday night he'd proven that

he could make Molly want him. What he wasn't sure
of was whether or not she'd get there on her own,
without an added push from him. It had never mattered to him before whether a woman desired him,
but with Molly, things were different.

Everything was different.

Maybe it was the pressure of last week, or perhaps
the simplicity of life in Payne, Massachusetts, that
was having this effect on him. For reasons he couldn't
begin to define, he needed to know that Molly wanted
him. Monday, she'd been trapped by her own impulsiveness. She'd taken his offer because her sense of
honor had demanded it. He was absolutely certain of
that.

But it wasn't enough. Sam wanted her to look at
him, her eyes bright with passion, her lips slightly
parted, her fingers trembling and her heart racing. He
wanted her to feel the same gut-clenching need he
felt as he watched her. Until this morning, he wasn't
certain it could ever happen.

If he'd had any doubts, she'd erased them when
she launched into that ludicrous little speech about
not letting their relationship go to their heads.

He nearly told her then that she'd been in his head
since the day they'd met. He'd been gambling he
could get Molly to admit that her frustration with him
in editorial meetings had little to do with his direction
for the *Sentinel,* and a lot to do with the tug of physical attraction they'd both been battling. Though he
would have preferred to avoid the spectacle she'd
caused with that damned ad, it had given him the
opening he'd needed to pursue her. He'd had a hell

of a time avoiding his sister's and sister-in-law's questions this week in Boston, but he'd managed to extricate himself with a minimal hassle.

This morning's conversation had been eye-opening. Molly, he sensed, was the kind of woman who liked to control her relationships. She chose men who didn't push her buttons. She found strays, took them in, cleaned them up, and turned them loose without ever suffering even a twinge of remorse.

No wonder he made her so nervous, he thought with a dry grin. His attention was drawn by the sound of Molly's voice carrying above the cheering crowd. Her duck was losing badly in the opening heat of the day-long event. She should have taken his advice when she'd insisted on picking the scraggiest-looking duck from the pen. He dropped his empty coffee cup in a wastebasket and headed for Molly.

"Run!" she yelled at her duck as she waved her arms toward the finish line. "Run!"

Sam joined her at the fence and slid an arm around her waist. "I think it's a lost cause."

She gave him a sharp look. "It's never a lost cause, Sam."

He tipped his head toward the field where the ducks were weaving their way across open grass toward a pile of corn which formed a makeshift finish line. Molly's duck didn't seem particularly interested in the feed. The duck races, Sam had learned, were conducted at several levels and heats. Local farmers had ducks available for sponsorship for people like Molly who wanted to compete but didn't have a duck of their own. The big event took place later in the day

when competitors who had raised and trained their
own ducks competed in a multi-heat event. The rest
of the festival tents housed music, concessions and
some agricultural interest exhibits which helped dis-
perse the large crowd over the expansive fair grounds.
''It's a scrawny duck,'' Sam told Molly. ''I told you
not to pick a scrawny duck.''

''You don't always have to be—''

''Molly?'' A soft voice attracted Sam's attention.
He glanced over his shoulder to find an auburn-haired
woman with two children in tow watching them with
avid curiosity. ''We've been looking for you all
morning.''

''Aunt Molly!'' The youngest of the two children
raced forward and hurled her small body at Molly.

''Hiya, sprout,'' Molly said as she scooped up the
child. She smiled at the woman. ''Colleen. I didn't
expect you guys to come this early.'' She nodded her
head toward Sam. ''This is Sam Reed.''

Colleen gave Sam a probing look. ''I guessed.''

''This is my sister, Colleen,'' Molly said. She indicated the older child. ''This is my niece, Megan,
and this—'' she hugged the child in her arms closer
''—is Kelly.''

''Aunt Molly,'' Kelly demanded. ''Dad's gonna
get me a baby duck for the kid races.''

Molly looked at Megan who was clinging to her
mother's hand and staring at Sam. ''What about you,
Megan? Are you going to get a duck, too?''

Megan shook her head. Red curls bounced against
her round cheeks. Kelly made a disgusted sound.
''Megan's chicken.''

Megan gave her sister a belligerent look. "Am not."

"Are, too."

"Am *not!*"

"Girls!" Colleen said sharply. "Stop it."

Kelly patted Molly's shoulder. "Dad says if you're gonna get a duck, you gotta pick it up. Megan doesn't wanna."

"That doesn't mean I'm scared," Megan insisted.

"Enough." Colleen said with a maternal authority that effectively squelched the budding argument. "If Megan doesn't want a duck, I can't say I blame her. Molly's the only member of this family who's ever been willing to handle one." She glanced at Sam. "Sorry to subject you to this. I'm sure you had other plans for the day."

He shook his head. "I've got siblings. I'm used to it." He extended a hand to her. "It's nice to meet you."

"Nice to meet you, too." She glanced at Molly. "I'm a little surprised."

"I'll bet," Molly drawled. A loud cheer from the crowd signaled the end of the race. Molly looked at the field to discover her duck still lingering by the outside fence. "I lost," she said unnecessarily.

Kelly leaned forward to look at Molly's duck. "It's a skinny duck."

Sam turned to Molly with smug satisfaction. "See?"

She glared at him. "Cute."

Colleen was watching the exchange with keen intent. "Er, Molly, are you planning on joining us all for lunch?"

Molly nodded. "Of course. There's no way I'm going to miss Mama's chicken salad. She only makes it once a year."

Kelly looked at Sam. "Is he coming, too?"

"Yes."

Kelly grinned. "Mama says he's your boyfriend."

Colleen blushed. Sam laughed. Molly shook her head. "You should know by now, Colleen, that they will tell me everything."

"We had a long conversation at dinner last night about the ad."

"I'm sure you did," Molly told her.

"They were excited about seeing you today."

"I'm surprised you're here this early. You usually come with Mama and Dad in time for lunch."

"We came early so Todd could arrange for Kelly's duck," Colleen explained.

"I'm getting a fat one," the younger child stated. "Not a skinny one like yours."

Molly shook her head. "There's nothing wrong with skinny ducks, Kel."

"'Cept they lose," Kelly stated bluntly.

Sam crossed his arms and leaned one hip against the fence. Molly frowned at him. "Smugness is unbecoming."

"You just can't stand it when I'm right."

She rolled her eyes and looked at Colleen. "So are you staying for the rest of the morning?"

"I don't think so. It's hard on the girls."

Molly lowered Kelly to the ground. "I understand."

Colleen turned to Sam. "You're welcome to join us for lunch, Sam."

"It'll be a little wild," Molly assured him. "My niece Katie is turning five this week, so we usually have the family celebration the day of the duck races."

Colleen added, "We'd love to have you. Everyone's eager to meet you."

He could well imagine. "I'm planning on it," Sam assured Colleen. Molly's audible groan gave him undue satisfaction.

TWO HOURS LATER, Sam and Molly crested a small hill and stepped straight into what had once been Sam's personal idea of paradise. Before he lived with Edward Reed's family, his mother had moved from one place to the next, living off credit, charity, and cunning. The large, wealthy Reed family had provided Sam with a sense of stability, but he'd never enjoyed the unconditional support and love of family except from his two half siblings and, to his continued surprise, from his stepmother.

Never feeling he completely belonged to the world of the Reeds, Sam had turned inward, developing a strong sense of self and independence. The only birthday party he'd ever had was the one he'd thrown for himself when he was six years old. Three alley cats and a stray dog had come to share a honey bun he'd swiped from the corner market. Though the Reeds had taken him in and treated him well, they'd never been big on celebrations. That was why, he'd reasoned long ago, his half sister loved planning weddings. They gave her something to anticipate.

And after what he'd gone through this past week, he thought bitterly as he surveyed the scene before him. The stark reality of the difference between his life and Molly's made him feel as if he'd been hit head-on by a freight train.

In his childhood dreams, birthdays had looked like this. Green and orange crepe paper colorfully wrapped the trunks of the large oaks near the expanse of lawn where the Flynns had gathered for lunch. The lawn was dotted with blankets and baskets where other families had climbed the rise to take a break from the crowds and the noise of the festival during the height of the day. Someone had tied helium balloons in clusters to several low-lying shrubs. The sounds of childish laughter carried above the low rumble of the crowd noise.

Sam hadn't understood until recently why Taylor's plans for his own birthday next week were making him feel so squeamish, but looking over the festive scene of Molly's family made his stomach clench and his mood sour. Molly had made it clear that morning that she expected an explanation for his whereabouts last week. She deserved one.

And having seen this, he wondered how in the hell he was supposed to tell her when he knew his answers would shock, and probably disgust her.

Deliberately, he shoved aside the grim thoughts and forced himself to concentrate on the moment at hand.

After meeting Colleen, Molly and Sam had spent

the morning circulating among the burgeoning crowds at the duck races. Sam had taken his share of good-natured ribbing over Molly's personal ad, and she handled the jibes and soft barbs with effortless grace. The only tense moment had come when they'd encountered Fred Cobell and his wife near the VIP tent. Cobell had given Sam a bitter look and said, "So, Reed, decided to see how the rest of us live?"

Sam slung a casual arm across Molly's shoulder. "Molly is showing me around."

Cobell's gaze shifted to Molly. "I've got a friend at the county clerk's office. She says you were asking some questions over there yesterday."

Molly nodded. "Just doing my job, Mayor. The *Sentinel* is going to cover the transportation hub development as comprehensively as we can."

"It's big news," Sam added.

Cobell's eyes had narrowed. "It's the best thing to happen to this town in a long time. The economic benefits are enormous."

"That's why the *Sentinel* is covering it," Sam said, non-committal.

The mayor crossed his arms over his ample chest and looked down his narrow nose at Molly. "Don't go looking for trouble, Molly," he said, his warning clear.

Molly raised an eyebrow. "Do you think there's trouble to be found?"

The mayor ignored her question. He gave Sam a knowing smirk. "You know, Reed, if you were this determined to learn what small-town life is like, you could have asked me. I'm sure we could have arranged something more, er, accommodating for you.''

Though he could have been talking about Sam's attendance at the duck races, his badly veiled reference to Molly was unmistakable. Sam had to squelch a biting retort. Instead, he gave Cobell a glacial look and replied, ''I like to make my own choices. It's more gratifying.''

Cobell's wife was pulling on his arm, urging him toward the VIP tent. He gave Sam a final glance and muttered, ''Carl told me you're committed to bringing some changes to the *Sentinel,* Reed. I'm counting on that.''

As Cobell followed his wife through the entrance of the VIP tent, Molly gave Sam a speculative look. ''I don't like him,'' she said. ''I've never liked him.''

''Me neither,'' Sam told her. ''But right now, he's useful. Investigating this story is going to get a lot tougher if he quits giving us access to information.''

Molly nodded thoughtfully. ''That's true enough,'' she concurred. ''But don't you think that association with me is going to make him suspicious? You didn't miss his innuendo, did you?''

''You mean the part about experiencing small-town life with you being messy?''

*''Unaccommodating,''* she said. ''Not messy. I'm sure Fred Cobell thinks you're an idiot for putting up with me.''

''Yeah. I caught that.''

''He meant it as a threat, you know. He's not going to trust you as much as he did before. He's resented me since his first election bid.''

"It may shock you to hear this, Molly, but Fred Cobell doesn't even register on my radar screen when I make decisions. I've got other priorities."

That had effectively closed the subject. It had taken Sam a while to shake his lingering bad mood, but Molly had goaded him out of it by introducing him to the town's blue ribbon winners in the festival's culinary tent. Sam had tasted enough assorted pies and confections to put him on a sugar high. Molly laughed at him when he'd told her that, indicating her plan had been to dull his senses with chocolate and sweets before she exposed him to her family.

Now, as they crested the rise, Sam took in the festive scene with trepidation. On their way up the hill, Molly had explained that her father was part owner of the large cranberry farm that bordered the fairgrounds. Most of the families and their employees in the ownership group used the hill's vantage point to pull away from the large crowd and the fairgrounds during the noon hour. Molly's entire family—all four sisters, their husbands, their kids, and her parents— would be present for the birthday gathering.

The thought made Sam nervous.

Molly's chief concern about his proposition earlier in the week had been breaking the news to her family. She was close to them, he knew, and she wouldn't be comfortable deceiving them. As far as Sam was concerned, the only duplicity about their relationship was the insinuation that Molly's ad had been a simple lover's quarrel. But Molly, he knew, was struggling with both her pride and her inherent openness. For weeks she'd been expressing her frustrations with him to her family and friends. She'd have to swallow her pride now and let them believe that she'd been involved with him.

Sam was anxious to see how she handled it.

"Sam?" Molly laid a hand on his sleeve.

"Hmm?"

Her head tipped in the direction of a large maple tree where blankets were spread with a mind-boggling quantity of food. "Incoming maternal unit. You're on."

"What?"

"My mother," she clarified.

Sam glanced at the tree. A plump woman, gray-haired and pleasant-faced, bustled toward them. Clad in a simple blue dress and wiping her hands on a dish towel, she had a warm smile and her daughter's intelligent gaze.

"Molly." She dried her hands as she hurried toward them. "You are late." The smile in her eyes undermined the severity of the rebuke. "Working too hard again, no doubt. What is there to learn at the duck races that you don't already know?"

With a warm laugh, Molly embraced her mother. "It's different every year, Mom. And you know it. Stop nagging."

"Katie was worried you wouldn't come."

"Katie knows better," she told her.

Her mother released her and looked at Sam. "This is the reason you're late?" she asked.

Sam grinned at her. "Guilty. This is my first duck races festival. Molly was showing me around." He extended his hand. "I'm Sam Reed."

Molly's mother took his hand in both of hers. "I'm Fiona Flynn."

Sam glanced at Molly as he squeezed Fiona's hand. She was worrying her lower lip with her teeth. He tossed his arm around her shoulders. "Thanks for letting me come this afternoon, Fiona. I know it's a family affair."

"Hah—the boys will be glad to have you." Fiona's eyes sparkled like her daughter's. "My husband and my daughters' husbands always complain about the ratio." She dropped his hand and beamed at Molly. "Besides, after Monday's paper, everyone's been dying to meet him." She clucked her tongue. "You've been avoiding phone calls."

"Mom, it's not—"

Fiona shook her head. "Never mind. I'm just glad you're here." She looped her arm through Sam's. "My girls tell me you've been in Payne several weeks. Is that so?"

He felt Molly's shoulders tense, so he gave her a slight squeeze before he dropped his arm. This was going better than he'd hoped. Colleen had been warm and accepting that morning, and now he seemed to have won over Fiona. The rest of the family couldn't be far behind. "I guess it has been a while," he said. "I haven't been counting." He slanted Molly a warm look. "I've had other things on my mind."

Fiona chuckled. "I suppose you have."

"Molly has a way of distracting me," he admitted.

Molly muttered something beneath her breath. If she could get away with it, he was guessing, she'd like to kick him in the shin. As far as he was concerned, however, the price she was paying for that personal ad was nothing compared to the intense grilling he'd taken from his family yesterday.

"Aunt Molly!"

A green-and-orange bundle of energy came racing across the lawn and hurled herself into Molly's arms. With a warm laugh, she picked the child up and spun her around. "Katie-Did. How does it feel to be five?"

"Better'n four," Katie assured her. Clad in a green sweater and orange jeans, her little body crackled with animation. Her pale hair lay in two neat braids, each threaded with multicolored ribbons. She wore a blue beaded necklace. Purple high-top sneakers completed the outrageous ensemble.

Molly dropped a kiss to her forehead before she set her down. "No kidding?"

Katie held fast to Molly's hand. "Yeah. I got a tractor."

Molly laughed. "A tractor? Isn't that a little big for you?"

"It's a *little* tractor." Katie gave Sam a curious look.

"Oh, I see," Molly assured her.

From behind the house, a woman who looked like an older, pregnant version of Molly made her way toward them. She was extremely pregnant, he noted, unsure why the sudden realization bothered him. He compared the emerging dynamics here with his last family gathering, Ben and Amy's wedding reception. His sister, who had planned countless weddings—including the five of her own she'd called off—had insisted on having the reception at the yacht club. The only people who'd felt more out of place than Sam were Amy and her parents.

Eileen picked her way slowly across the yard. One hand rested on her swollen belly, the other shaded her eyes from the bright afternoon sun. "Molly, hi."

"Hey, Eileen. This munchkin tells me she's got a tractor. Isn't Hutch being a little ambitious?"

When Eileen laughed, the sound had a weightless quality that drew Sam's attention. It was the same unfettered laugh as Molly's. This, he imagined, must be the benefit of a healthy family. Eileen brushed a strand of dark hair behind her ear as she glanced at Katie. "It's one of those pedal things," she said in answer to Molly's question. "She's so fascinated with Dad's riding mower that Hutch thought she'd like it."

"It's green, like Grandpa's," Katie announced.

"Your favorite color," Molly said. "How did your dad know you wanted green?"

"'Cause I told him." She looked pointedly at Sam. "Kelly and Megan says he's your boyfriend, Aunt Molly. Is he?"

"Katie," Eileen smoothly interjected, "why don't you go back to play with your cousins? I think Daddy almost has the hot dogs ready."

"Okay," Katie agreed, then looked at Sam again. "*Are* you Aunt Molly's boyfriend?"

Molly coughed. Sam grinned at the child and squatted down so he was at eye level with her. He extended his hand. "I'm Sam Reed. I'm a friend of your aunt's."

Katie's eyebrows drew together in a curious frown. "But are you her *boy*friend?"

"What do you know about boyfriends?" he asked her.

"I got one," she said. "His name is Steve. He's in my class."

"I see. How come Steve's your boyfriend?"

She thought the question over, then shrugged. "'Cause he's the boy I like best, I guess. He's pretty good at coloring, but his writing stinks."

Sam nodded solemnly. "I think your aunt says the same thing about my writing."

"Really?"

"Yep. So maybe I am her boyfriend."

That made the child giggle. Eileen gave her daughter a nudge. "Go back to Daddy, honey. We'll be along in a minute."

After admonishing Molly not to forget her present, Katie beamed at Sam, then skipped away. Eileen looked at Molly. "Since you've forgotten to introduce me, I'll do it myself." The light in her eyes took the sting out of the rebuke. She turned to Sam. "I'm Eileen. It's nice to meet you, Mr. Reed."

"Sam, please," he said. "Nobody calls me Mr. Reed after hours."

"You should hear what they call you behind your back," Molly quipped.

Sam shot her a knowing look. "And you all think I don't know it?"

Eileen's hand moved over the swell of her stomach. "Everyone was, er, intrigued on Monday," she said carefully. "That ad—"

He grinned at her. "You know what Molly's temper is like," he said dismissively. Beside him, he could feel Molly bristle. If he dared look at her, he was sure she'd have the same sour expression she'd given him when he'd called her "babe" at the office. "After the argument we had in an editorial meeting last Friday, I was surprised she let me off that easy."

Eileen raised her eyebrows and looked at Molly. "Really?"

Molly managed a slight nod. Sam retrieved the large package from her and tucked it under his arm. "I don't know about you," he said, "but I'm ready for lunch."

Molly frowned at him. "You just ate the equivalent of four pies at the culinary tent."

"I'm a man, Molly," he said, giving her a deliberately heated look. "Dessert doesn't satisfy all my hungers."

And before Molly could respond, her family swept them in the direction of the party.

WITH A FROWN, Molly studied Sam's profile. He was playing duck-duck-goose with her ten nieces. Seated in the tight circle, he had all ten girls obviously charmed. He seemed relaxed and at ease, and Molly was trying to assimilate this image of him with the irascible, inflexible man she'd seen at the *Sentinel*— and with the man who spent his weekends working on a vintage sailboat. In his green shirt and khaki trousers, he looked casual but elegant as the soft breeze tousled his dark hair. For a man used to country club parties and sophisticated entertainments, he'd handled the morning and boisterous afternoon with remarkable grace.

She had to give him that.

He'd seemingly had just one uncomfortable moment. They had followed Fiona and Eileen the rest of the way up the hill to find the large Flynn clan in full swing. Molly's four brothers-in-law stood around a charcoal grill with her father, while her four sisters sat at a picnic table and supervised their children—all girls. The running joke in the Flynn family was that no baby would dare be born a boy when he'd be outnumbered ten to one by his female cousins.

As Sam had glided to a halt he found himself the focus of her sisters' curious looks, but had quickly recovered. Flashing Molly a bright smile, he had retrieved a root beer from a nearby cooler and said, "My kind of party. The chicks outnumber the guys by more than three to one." The collective laugh he'd won from her family gave him instant entrée into their tightly knit clan. He pressed a diet soda into Molly's hand, then strolled away to join the men.

Leaving her, Molly thought irritably, to wonder how he knew she drank diet soda, and to deal with the pending interrogation from her sisters. She was surprised to find that he had, indeed, been right that she'd have no reason to lie about her relationship with him. She'd answered every question truthfully—from the way she'd met him, to how much he annoyed her at work, to why she'd run the ad in the morning paper. As he had predicted, her sisters had drawn their own conclusions. That, too, had irritated her—as if he'd taken something valuable from her. She'd always been able to turn to her sisters for advice, consolation, and support. Under normal circumstances, they would have been her safe haven on Monday when she'd seen the ad in the paper. Her plan had been to submit her resignation to Sam, then head to her sister Eileen's where she could eat chocolate chip cookies and talk ugly about the man who'd ruined her life at the *Sentinel*. But Sam had surprised her with his insistence and persistence. Her Flynn sense of honor had urged her to accept his offer. And one simple kiss that still tingled on her lips had shown her just how dicey it would be to keep her heart intact. When he'd neatly ducked the issue of his sudden disappearance for the last few days, she'd seen that passing look of stark loneliness in his gaze—the same look that had made it impossible for her to turn away from him in the first place.

Like the stray cat, he'd learned to deal with life's misfortunes by isolating himself. Whatever he'd been through in the past week had left an indelible impression, and whereas Molly would have turned to her vast network of family and friends for support, Sam shut people out.

That, she instinctively knew, was his style. Given what few facts she knew about his life and his strange assimilation into the Reed clan, she wasn't terribly surprised. Sam never got entangled. He never allowed things to get messy. No strings. No roots. No commitments. Not in work and not in life. When his job in Payne was through, he'd move on, back to a life of global travel, multi-billion-dollar deal brokering, and high-society entertainments.

And he'd be through with her, too.

Molly, on the other hand, was rooted here in a rural

community that made an annual event of duck races. She could not imagine leaving that behind. She'd decided that any relationship she might have with Sam would end in heartbreak. The choice she now weighed was the balance between the risk of a broken heart and the risk of never knowing what would happen if she tried to chase away Sam's lingering loneliness. It was the kind of choice that screamed for heart-to-heart conversations and sisterly advice—things Molly had learned to depend on. But now Sam stood between Molly and her sisters, her bargain with him precluding her from coming completely clean with them.

Fortunately, the meal and the festivities of Katie's birthday had turned some of the attention away from the novelty of Sam, and as her family had spread out among lawn chairs and picnic blankets, she had found herself seated alone with him. He asked questions, prodded her for stories about her family, and listened attentively—actively, even. He seemed fascinated by tales of Molly's and her sisters' childhood and adolescent experiences, and of her nieces' escapades. She noticed that he constantly found reasons to touch her. He'd brush a curl behind her ear or trace a finger along the veins on the back of her hand. Each little touch, each caress, stirred the embers of the passion that had been burning in her since Monday.

And with every question, every soft laugh, every curious look in his eyes, Molly had fallen for him just a little harder.

Feeling unreasonably irritable, Molly found a seat

at the picnic table where she could watch her nieces giggling with Sam on the verdant lawn.

She'd be a fool to fall for Sam, she'd told herself countless times, repeating the argument to herself regularly since his kiss that morning. Yet it still failed to convince her. Sam was tasting pies and listening to advice and comments about the *Sentinel* when Molly hit upon the reason she felt so wary with him. Though her friends and family had often accused her of falling in love too hard and too fast, she'd always known the truth. The guys she fell for were really just projects. They'd needed her. And she'd enjoyed being needed.

As a rule, she didn't go for men like I've-got-the-world-by-the-tail Sam Reed. Sam didn't need anybody or anything. And falling in love with him would be utterly and stupendously stupid. For the first time in her life, Molly almost wished she could simply indulge in a casual affair, fully comfortable with the knowledge that when Sam's work in Payne was done, he'd climb into his private plane and fly out of her life.

But she couldn't. And she knew it. If she let herself fall for Sam, she'd end up nursing a colossal broken heart. So the question became, was he worth it?

Molly drummed her fingers on the table and watched him accept his role as the designated goose. He rose fluidly from the circle of girls and chased her niece, Emily, around the circle. Emily won easily— no doubt because Sam had tamed his strides to small steps that gave the six-year-old a significant advantage. At least, she mused as she watched the flex of his broad shoulders and his long-legged strides, no one could blame her for finding him sexy as sin.

And if she'd listened to her sisters weeks ago, she'd have seen this coming, but she'd been so sure....

It would have been so much easier if he'd simply accepted her resignation, she thought wearily. She'd contemplated quitting a dozen times, but in the back of her mind was the realization that she'd created this mess. That she had, indeed, through her own impulsiveness, caused him a considerable amount of embarrassment. And he'd taken it all in stride, letting her off the hook for little more than a couple of dinner dates and some mildly uncomfortable suppositions on the part of her friends and family.

She owed him.

And honor wouldn't let her squelch—even if he did make her stomach flutter and her pulse race. As if he sensed her scrutiny, he looked her way and grinned at her.

Molly's heart thudded a little harder.

"Problems?"

Molly glanced up as her sister Colleen handed her a bottle of soda and took the seat next to her at the picnic table.

"Not problems, exactly," she mumbled. Across the lawn, Katie and her cousins were laughing in delight as they tackled Sam to the ground.

"You have the look," Colleen said.

"What look?"

"The some-man-is-turning-you-inside-out look."

"Oh." She took a long sip of her soda. "That look."

Colleen's gaze followed hers to the spot beneath the oak tree. "He seems—interesting."

"You mean in that superpowerful, extremely wealthy corporate magnate kind of way?"

Colleen's eyebrows lifted. "Did I hit a nerve?"

Molly winced. "No. Sorry. It's just been a long couple of days."

"I'll bet. Which is why enquiring minds want to know why you've been avoiding our calls."

"I've been really busy," Molly hedged.

Colleen gave her a shrewd look. "Not *that* busy. You're never that busy, Mol." She shook her head and a dark red wave of hair tumbled over her shoulder. "Something's going on between you and this guy."

Molly couldn't suppress a slight smile. "I don't suppose you got the idea from that asinine personal ad, did you?"

Her sister laughed. "I have to admit, that was a little over the top, even for you. How mad were you to do something like that?"

"It's a long story."

"I can imagine. I can also imagine that Sam didn't especially appreciate your sense of humor. Was he super pissed or what?"

"Actually, no." She shook her head. "Believe it or not, he let me off kind of easy."

"Seriously?" Her sister pressed. "Todd would have *killed* me for that."

"Before or after he finished worshipping the ground you walk on?"

"He does not." Molly gave her sister a knowing

look. Colleen laughed. "Okay, he sort of does, but don't tell him I know. He thinks I'm oblivious."

"You're safe with me."

"Still, he would've been seriously annoyed if I'd pulled a stunt like that. I mean, it's so *public*, Molly. Couldn't you think of something a little less dramatic to tell him you were steamed?"

"I told you, it wasn't supposed to get printed."

"What *did* you two fight about anyway?"

"A story I wanted to write."

Colleen shook her head, her eyes twinkling. "I should have known." She drank some of her soda. "The way you've been complaining about this man for the past few weeks, it was just a matter of time—"

"I wouldn't say that."

"Sure it was. You've talked of little else since Carl brought him in. I have to admit, all that protesting was beginning to sound suspicious."

"Colleen—"

"Come on, Molly. I've seen you through, what, five major heartbreaks?"

"At least."

Colleen nodded. "I know the signs. When you start talking nonstop about anything other than the paper, things are getting serious."

"The paper is the biggest part of my life. Sam's making a lot of changes." Molly frowned. "He bugs the crud out of me."

"I know. Todd annoyed me at first, too." Colleen shook her head again. "And if you remember, Hutch bugged the hell out of Eileen. We thought they'd never make it down the aisle. Eventually, you'll get over it.''

"I'm not so sure.''

"Some couples don't, you know. They bicker all the time.''

"That's a cheery thought.''

"They also get to make up a lot. Passion, Molly. It's got a lot of different faces.''

That's precisely what Sam had said. "I guess it does.''

"So, how long were you planning to keep us in the dark about him?" Colleen asked. "You know we were bound to find out sooner or later.''

Molly shrugged. "I don't know. It never came up.'' She shot a look at Eileen. "Is Eileen upset that I didn't say anything?" Their oldest sister was the most sensitive of the brood.

"I don't think so. If it had been any of the rest of us, we'd have spilled our guts weeks ago. But not you. Everyone knows you're more independent.''

"Hmm.'' She looked at Sam again. The game appeared to have ended. He had the ten little girls gathered in a tight circle where they were watching him with avid interest. With *that* voice, Molly thought, he could recite the preamble to the U.S. Constitution and women everywhere would fall under his spell.

"He's hot,'' Colleen said slowly, following the direction of her gaze. "In that brooding, man-of-the-earth kind of way.''

"What woman can resist a man who plays duck-duck-goose,'' Molly said.

"You've got a point there. I wouldn't have pictured the two of you together until I actually saw it. But the chemistry—Lord, Molly. The way he looks at you—it just sort of sizzles, you know? No wonder he's been making you nuts.''

''You don't have to sound so smug.''

''Hey, I told you weeks ago when you were venting about him that I thought you had it for him. If I'd seen you two together, I would have put money on it.''

Molly trailed a finger through the moisture on her soda bottle and studied the rivulets of condensation on the glass. ''I didn't know at the time,'' she confessed. ''It was only recently—''

''Molly?'' She started at the sound of Sam's voice. He placed one hand on her shoulder. ''Sorry,'' he said. ''Didn't mean to startle you.''

Colleen looked at Molly for several long seconds, then stood to go. ''I didn't realize how late it was getting. We've got to get down to the grandstands or we won't have a seat for the final races.'' She extended her hand to Sam. ''It was very nice to meet you, Sam. I hope you're going to join us for the rest of the festival.''

''I wouldn't miss it.'' He gave her hand a quick squeeze.

Colleen smiled at Molly. ''Later this week,'' she said, ''we'll have lunch.''

''I'll try,'' Molly promised as her sister wandered off in search of her family. She finally looked at Sam. ''Hi.''

''Hi.'' He sat next to her. ''Everything okay?''

''Sure.''

"I had a feeling you were getting the third degree from your sister."

Her laugh was short. "You could say that. You were right though. Everyone bought it."

"And that makes you a little sad," he said with uncanny accuracy.

She wasn't sure why his insight made her uncomfortable. "Sort of."

"I understand."

His quiet assertion surprised her. There were depths to this man that she'd never even imagined. "How did you know?" she pressed.

He reached for her hand. "I've spent most of my life being part of, but not really belonging to, the Reed family. I know what it's like to be alone in a big group of people."

"I'm very close to my family."

"But you don't always feel like you fit in?"

She looked around where her siblings were packing up their belongings and their kids. The main event of the Duck Races Festival, the scholarship competition race, took place in the late afternoon. The Flynn clan would make their way to the grandstand where they'd find seats for the competition. "This makes me feel guilty."

"I told you to just tell them the truth."

"I did," she said carefully. "They didn't ask as much as they could have."

He nodded, skimming his thumb over her knuckles. "And it bothered you, didn't it?"

"Yes and no. I can't explain it."

"It's hard," he said, sliding his hand up her arm

to cup her elbow. He nudged her a little closer. "There's a fine line between wanting your privacy and wishing people cared enough to dig a little deeper."

She searched his expression. Though it showed nothing unusual, there was something in the statement Molly found inexplicably sad. "Sam—"

"Aunt Molly! Aunt Molly!" Katie came racing toward them across the hill.

"Does she run everywhere she goes?" Sam asked Molly seconds before the little girl hurled herself into Molly's arms.

Molly hugged Katie close and looked at Sam. "She got that from me."

"Aunt Molly, thank you for my ball and pole thing," she said referring to the tether ball set Molly had given her for her birthday. "I really like it."

"You're welcome, Katie-Diddle. I'm glad you're having a good birthday."

Katie squirmed loose, her attention fully on Sam. "Next time you come see me, if you come to my house, you can play with my—" She looked at Molly. "What's it called again?"

"Tether ball."

"Yeah. That." Katie turned back to Sam. "Dad said he'd set it up. I bet I could take ya'."

Sam laughed. The rich chuckle soothed Molly's shredded nerves like a glass of cognac. Sam braced his hands on his thighs and leaned over until his face was eye level with Katie's. "I don't know, I'm taller."

"But I'm quicker," she insisted.

''That may be true,'' he conceded. He stuck out his hand. ''Deal. Next time, we'll play tether ball.''

Katie grinned at him and gave his hand a hard shake. Her father called her name from across the hill. She gave Molly a quick kiss and said, ''Bye. Gotta go.'' She took off at a run toward her waiting parents.

Sam shook his head. ''Did you have that much energy when you were her age?''

''Are you kidding?'' Molly stood and picked up her empty soda bottle, deliberately casting off her lingering gray mood. She'd loved this festival for years. She wasn't about to let brooding thoughts spoil the sheer pleasure of the afternoon. ''I have that much energy now.''

''That's what I'm afraid of,'' he assured her. ''And counting on.''

# Chapter Eight

Sam and Molly followed the Flynns into the seating area where they had a decent vantage point for the final heats of the races. Kelly tapped Sam on the shoulder. "Hey, Sam? Wanna try my b'nocalars?" She extended the hot-pink binoculars to him. "You can see the ducks better."

Sam accepted the plastic binoculars. "Don't you need them?"

"Nah. You seen one duck, you've seen 'em all," she announced, indicating the medal she'd won in the heats earlier that day.

Her father pulled her back. "Bottom on the seat, Kel. Quit bugging Sam."

Sam was about to thank her for the binoculars when Katie's voice attracted the attention of the entire group. "Holy cow!" she exclaimed. "Who is that?"

All eyes turned in the direction of the child's pointed hand. A black limousine had stopped outside the gates of the fairgrounds. A party of three, one man and two women, was making its way toward the viewing stands. Other than their ostentatious black limousine, there was nothing remarkable about two members of the party. The man and one of the women were dressed casually in jeans and sweaters, blending in well with the rest of the crowd. But what had drawn Katie's attention and was gradually drawing the attention of the entire population of Payne was the flamboyantly dressed woman in a bright yellow designer suit. She wore orange boots and an orange straw hat bedecked with yellow ostrich feathers. She carried a yellow parasol and an orange patent leather purse. As she alighted from the limousine and scanned the crowd, a frown marred her elegant features.

Sam rolled his eyes in a combination of weary resignation and irritation. "That," he said, rising to his feet, "is my sister."

"SAM!" Taylor Reed rushed forward to hug her brother. "Sam, I'm glad we found you." She looked around at the large crowd. "This crowd's as big as you said it would be."

"You sound surprised," he drawled.

Taylor shook her head. "Pleasantly surprised. I called Amy last night and told her that since you described this event, I've been dying to see the ducks." She lowered her voice slightly. "And to meet your new friends."

Sam glanced at his brother who stood with one arm around his wife, just behind their flamboyant sister. "Ben."

"I tried to talk her out of it," Ben assured him. "You know how she is."

Taylor affected a flirtatious pout. "For your information, I happen to like ducks."

Molly, who had walked toward the entrance with Sam, was watching the spectacle with fascination. She'd always believed that most celebrities had a secret longing to disappear into the crowd, to shed the watchful eyes of the press and public. Taylor Reed showed no such inclination. In her outlandish costume, she had leapt onto center stage and was holding it with ease. "I assumed you had neglected to invite us along today because you thought we wouldn't enjoy it."

"I don't suppose it occurred to you," Sam said, his voice indulgent, "that maybe I was looking for a little privacy?"

Taylor laughed with a tone that surprised Molly. It was genuine and warm, lacking the brittle artificiality she'd heard in the laughter of other socialites. "Don't be ridiculous," she replied to Sam. "Of course it occurred to me. I just chose to ignore it."

Sam's smile was both benevolent and resigned. He liked his sister, despite or maybe even because of her flamboyance. "I should have known," he muttered.

Taylor nodded. "Indubitably. Besides—" the expression in her eyes softened as she squeezed Sam's arm "—I wasn't ready to let go of you yet." An unspoken bond between the two seemed to strengthen. Molly noted the exchange curiously.

Taylor then glanced at Molly. The soft look she'd given Sam was gone. In its place were curiosity and devilment. "This must be the one," she told her brother.

Molly took a deep breath and stuck out her hand. "Molly Flynn."

Taylor smiled—a wide, generous smile without a hint of guile—then gave her hand a firm shake. "Taylor Reed. You have no idea how glad I am to meet you."

Molly slid a glance at Sam. "Oh, really?"

Sam indicated his brother. "This is my brother, Ben, and his wife, Amy."

Molly shook their hands. Amy was studying her with rapt attention. "It's nice to meet you, Molly."

Amy looked around at the festivities with keen interest. "I can't believe I've lived in Boston for five years and never knew this was here."

"Journalistic coverage has always been local. Word-of-mouth draws the crowd," Sam told her.

"We had twelve thousand last year," Molly said curtly. "We're not trying to compete with the Superbowl, you know."

Amy glanced at Molly. "Sam says there's a scholarship involved here."

Surprised, Molly wondered how much Sam had told his family about today—and about her. "Yes," she said. She briefly explained the responsibilities of the students who entered the annual event and the motive behind the scholarship. "It might not be the National Merit Scholar Program," she said, "but we believe in it. These kids work very hard for this."

Ben's nod was thoughtful. "I can see why you'd want to get behind this."

Taylor seemed to grow impatient without the reins of the conversation firmly in her grasp. Twirling her parasol, she exclaimed with keen delight, "I'm guessing Sam's not in it for the ducks."

"Taylor—" Sam's voice carried a note of caution.

She swatted his arm lightly. "Well, you're not." She looked at Molly. "And now I know why."

Before Molly could respond, a loud voice on the intercom interrupted, urging spectators to take their seats before the first heat of the featured races. Taylor linked her arm through Molly's. "This is so exciting," she said. "I have always adored races, and I could never get Father to take me. He took Ben and Sam to the Derby once, but he wouldn't take me."

Behind her, Sam snorted. "He was afraid you'd embarrass us."

Taylor clucked her tongue. "Oh, hush, Sam," she admonished before turning back to Molly. "To be perfectly honest, I'm dying to know how in the world you tolerate him. He can be absolutely insufferable." Despite the harsh words, Taylor's expression was benevolent. The woman had a definite soft spot for her half brother.

The voice on the intercom interrupted again, and Sam urged them back toward the stands. Taylor kept her hold on Molly's arm. "You have to explain everything to me," she told Molly. "Sam says you're an absolute expert at this."

Molly frowned at him as he breezed past her and led the party back to their seats. Introductions were made, her family readily embracing Sam's family, and they all settled in for the evening's entertainment. Sam sat next to Molly and immediately reached for her hand. He cradled it tightly in his, watching the field with undue interest. Molly leaned toward his shoulder and whispered, "Did you invite your step-mother, too?"

He looked surprised. "This wasn't my idea. Taylor's the one who wanted to come."

"But you told her about it."

"She asked me why I was rushing back to Payne this weekend," he said, his tone pure innocence.

Molly jabbed him in the ribs. "Admit it, Sam. You were fascinated by the idea of the races and you wanted to find out what would happen if someone other than the people of Payne came to see them."

His eyes twinkled. "Maybe."

"Bet you she'll enjoy herself."

"What are you willing to bet?" he countered.

Molly saw a caution flag at the slightly baited question, but ignored it. "I don't know. Winner picks the prize."

"That could be dangerous."

"Maybe—if I weren't so sure I was going to win."

"What are you going to make me do if I lose?"

"Let me write the traditional piece about the duck races for the *Sentinel*'s Monday edition."

Sam thought it over. "All right."

His ready agreement made her suspicious. "That was too easy."

Satisfied, Molly relaxed. "Good."

He leaned a fraction closer to her, and she felt his warm breath on her neck. "Don't you want to know what I'm going to make you do if *I* win?"

"No," she said bluntly. "I don't think that's a good idea."

"Why not?"

"Because, as I told you this morning, I don't think we should let this go to our heads."

"Too late," he whispered. "It's in my head, and in my blood, and I want you, Molly." He reached up to tuck a strand of hair behind her ear. The brush of his fingers on her cheek sent goose bumps down her spine. "And whether you admit it or not, it's inevitable and you know it."

"FOUL," TAYLOR YELLED, and jumped to her feet. "Foul." She was pointing to the field where the ducks were running the second heat of the night. "Where's the referee? Where's the umpire?"

Amy Reed was laughing so hard her pretty features had flushed. "Taylor, sit down."

Kelly tugged on Taylor's jacket. "There is no referee. That's for football."

Taylor was not appeased. "But that duck crossed lanes. It was a deliberate foul."

"They're allowed to do that," Kelly said knowledgeably. "It's not like normal racing."

"Yeah," Megan chimed in. "There are no rules for the ducks. Only for the people who race 'em."

With an outraged huff, Taylor dropped back to her seat. "I liked that brown duck," she said. "He was a fighter."

Molly darted a glance at Sam. He sat beside her, still holding her hand tightly in his, his words from before the race ringing in her ears. As they settled into the event, Taylor's obvious enjoyment began to ease some of Molly's tension. She felt simultaneously relieved and let down.

Sam had not let go of her hand since the races began. She was unsure whether he was putting on a show for her family and his, or whether he genuinely wanted the contact. The thought frustrated her until she felt the gentle stroke of Sam's thumb across her knuckles. This was not, he assured her silently, part of the pretense. Fresh in her mind was the haunted look on Sam's face when he'd stood at her door last night. The surprise of finding him there, of seeing his exhaustion, had given way to a desire to ease the deep shadows she'd seen under his eyes. Before the day was through, she promised herself, she'd have answers to her questions.

But now he was studying the field, apparently ignoring his sister's avid and colorful commentary. "At least there's no betting on the races. Your sister would probably lose the family fortune."

"Thank God," he muttered. "I can only gamble so much in one day."

"The kids are enjoying her."

"Nearly everyone enjoys Taylor." His tone was pure benevolence.

On Molly's left, Taylor was still protesting on behalf of the brown duck as she looked through the bright pink binoculars. "He should have won."

"Too skinny," Kelly told her. "Skinny ducks don't win."

Sam jabbed Molly in the ribs. "Told you."

She gave him a killing look. "Funny, Sam."

The ducks finished the heat, and Taylor dropped

the binoculars to her lap. "Drat. I was pulling for the brown one."

Molly's father leaned forward and began to explain to Taylor the intricacies of duck racing. The rest of the family chimed in with their own expert tips.

Molly listened as the chatter around her grew. Sam's family had joined hers with an apparent ease that left her feeling confused and inexplicably frustrated. It was easier to picture him leaving Payne without having seen this melding of their lives.

The air turned slightly chill as the sun began to set. Sam's hand felt warm where it still cradled hers. He rubbed the back of her knuckles again with his thumb. "You look perplexed," he said softly.

"They're not what I expected," she confessed. "Your family, I mean."

His expression turned slightly amused. "They're usually not. Especially Taylor."

"I like her."

"You sound surprised."

Molly winced. "I guess I am, a little. I'm guilty of making assumptions I shouldn't have."

"Thanks for admitting it." He studied her for a minute. "And if it makes you feel any better, I am, too."

Molly lifted her eyebrows. Sam nodded. "Your family. I had other expectations."

"Oh?"

He shrugged. "I can't explain it. I didn't think they'd take me in so readily."

That made Molly laugh. Poor Sam obviously didn't have a clue about the Flynns. "That's what we do,

Sam. Some families collect money or art or antiques. We collect people. That's what it means to be a Flynn.''

He thought that over. Finally, he glanced past Molly to where Taylor was involved in conversation with Kelly. "How much longer are you going to give her before you grill her about the birthday party next week?''

If the stroke of his thumb hadn't been making her pulse race, she might have laughed. Molly extricated her hand. "Another hour, I think. When she's really intoxicated from the warm soda and hot dogs, I'll nail her.''

Sam's mouth lifted into a grin. "I want you to go with me," he said softly. "I'd like it very much if you would. I know it's short notice.''

Molly considered that. "You didn't on Tuesday.''

"I do now.''

"What changed your mind?''

"Seeing you and Taylor together," he said. "And other things.''

"Sam—''

He shook his head. "I guess you could say I had different expectations.''

Molly wasn't sure how to take him. "You thought I wouldn't make a good impression.''

He frowned. "What gave you that idea?''

"I don't know. You seemed reluctant for me to meet your family.''

"That had nothing to do with you," he told her.

Would he ever stop surprising her? she wondered.

He'd returned his attention to the field. Molly studied his profile. "Sam?"

"Hmm?" He kept his gaze trained on the starting line where the ducks were being positioned for another heat.

"Are you ever going to tell me where you were last week?"

When he turned to her, the expression in his eyes was so raw, it stole Molly's breath. "Later. I'm enjoying the ducks."

She hesitated, but her curiosity gave way to his obvious need for time. She sent him a quick grin to ease the tension. "Can I quote you on that?"

Sam chuckled. "All right. I concede. You can write the piece."

"Thank God you've finally seen reason."

"*If,*" he added, "we run it parallel with the historical perspective."

She nodded. "Deal. I think that's fair."

His eyes twinkled. "Then you're going to have a very long day tomorrow, Molly, because in case you've forgotten, you've got a four o'clock deadline."

"I'm very good under pressure," she assured him.

SAM INSISTED on driving Molly's car home that night. He wasn't going to risk his life by letting her drive in the heavy festival traffic. Molly had grumbled, but had finally relinquished the keys. They'd sat in companionable silence while Sam negotiated his way through the stream of cars exiting the parking lot.

He liked that about Molly. She didn't need to fill

up empty space with idle chatter. He found that sexy, he realized. He slanted her a quick look. The moon was full, and it bathed her hair and face with the luminescent glow he'd seen in the boathouse. Now, as then, it awakened visions of seeing and touching her skin, of tasting her secrets and of finding all the places on her body that would make her moan.

Sam shifted in his seat as the stream of images had its predictable effect. Molly's fingers were tapping an idle rhythm on her thigh. They were long and slender, and he could still feel their imprint on his hand.

The heat in his body spiked up another notch. To-night, he promised himself silently—just as he had when he'd sat in the grandstands with her, just as he had when he'd watched her with her family, just as he had when he'd seen her leaning over that fence and cheering for a duck—tonight, he would coax that look out of her. He'd see her turn to him with an invitation in her gaze that would finally assuage the hunger he'd been harboring for weeks.

As he finally escaped the parking lot traffic, Sam shifted into high gear. Beside him, Molly sighed and leaned back in her seat. "Thanks, Sam," she said softly.

He glanced at her, his eyebrow raised. "For what?"

"For driving. For being so wonderful with my nieces. For—" Molly hesitated.

"For?"

She took a shaky breath. "For not being who I thought you were." She looked out the window. "I'm embarrassed. It's not like me to jump to conclusions.''

"I was in your territory," he told her. "I understand."

"You didn't seem to understand when I was arguing with you these past few weeks."

His lips twitched. "That's because you turned me on."

She frowned at him. "Sam—"

"You did." He turned into the long street that led to her house. "Anybody ever tell you you're cute when you're angry?"

"Not and live to tell about it," she muttered.

Sam laughed. "I'll bet."

"For what it's worth, though, I like your family."

"I'm glad."

"Your sister is…"

"Don't worry," Sam assured her. "You're not the first person to say that Taylor defies description."

"I'm beginning to see why you're nervous about this birthday party. Is she always so flamboyant?"

Sam parked in front of Molly's brownstone. "For as long as I've known her," he said as he opened his door. He rounded the car in four quick strides and helped Molly onto the curb. He liked the way she threaded her fingers through his and kept her grip on his hand as they walked up the sidewalk. It felt quaint and old-fashioned. And very much like something people did in Payne, Massachusetts.

With little effort Sam could picture himself walking down the tree-lined streets holding her hand, wading through the leaves that littered the sidewalks at this time of year. With Molly, he imagined, it would be the same twenty years from now. She'd still have that fire in her eyes and that adorable tilt to her mouth. She'd still argue with him. And she'd still have the power to make him want her. The image caught him off guard. He wasn't accustomed to imagining longevity or permanence. That was a luxury he'd never been able to afford.

Molly took her keys from Sam and opened her front door. As the light from the foyer spilled across their feet, she looked at him. "Sam—"

In the dim light, he couldn't read her expression. "Yes?"

"I want you to come in," Molly said simply.

Sam felt a rush of satisfaction as he pushed open the door. "I thought you'd never ask."

TWENTY MINUTES LATER, he sat with his feet propped on Molly's coffee table, a cup of hot chocolate in his hand, and Molly curled against his arm while a warm fire crackled in the fireplace. He'd experienced world-class entertainment that held far less appeal, he decided.

Molly turned toward him, her look piercing. "Okay, Sam, out with it. I'm out of patience!"

He gritted his teeth. "There really isn't—"

"Uh-uh. You don't get to disappear for four days without telling me where you've been. This getting involved thing was your idea—not mine."

He cursed beneath his breath and plunked his mug down. "It's family stuff. It doesn't bear—"

"You promised," she reminded him.

"I did not."

"You did."

"When?"

"Doesn't matter. You promised you'd tell me later."

"I said later. I didn't say anything about tonight."

"I say it is later." She lowered her head and studied him in the firelight. "What's the big deal? Were you with the other woman?"

Sam frowned and removed his arm from around her shoulders. She couldn't possibly know what this would cost him. "Cute," he said as he surged to his feet. He grabbed his mug and headed for the kitchen.

Behind him, Molly scrambled off the sofa. "Sam—" He kept walking. She caught up to him and blocked his entrance to the kitchen. "Sam, wait. What is the matter with you?"

He could feel the tension rising in his shoulders as he looked at her. What he wanted to do, what he'd wanted to do every night that week, was to take Molly to bed so he could forget. He could bury himself in her warmth, in her sweetness, in her vibrancy. Then all the aggravation and sourness of the past few days, hell, of most of his life would melt away, just for a moment. He knew, absolutely knew, that making love to Molly would do that. She'd consume him, and for an instant she'd obliterate everything else.

Molly's expression registered her concern. When she laid a hand on his chest, he felt the soft contact all the way to his core. "Sam?"

He hesitated, shocking himself with the realization that he *wanted* to tell her. The thought sent him reeling. He couldn't remember the last time he'd wanted to tell anyone something as personal as what he'd been through this week. Life had taught him the value of privacy. The fact that he was tempted to unload his burden at Molly's sympathetic feet made him feel inexplicably vulnerable and uneasy. With a soft groan, he covered her hand with his and tugged her toward the kitchen.

Molly followed wordlessly, as if she sensed his conflict. It was one of the things he liked best about her. She knew the value of unspoken communication.

Sam dumped the remaining contents of his mug in the sink and turned to put his hands on Molly's waist. He lifted her easily and sat her on the counter. With one step, he stood between her legs, his face at her eye level. Molly's eyes searched his as she placed her hands on his shoulders. "Talk to me," she urged. "Something's wrong."

Dreadfully wrong, he concurred. Embarrassingly wrong. So wrong she couldn't possibly imagine what this was costing him. Sam drew in a ragged breath. "My mother called Tuesday."

Molly gently stroked his shoulder. "And?"

"And it's the first time I've spoken to her since she handed me over to Edward."

Understanding dawned in her gaze. "I see."

Sam shook his head. "I doubt it."

"Did she call because of the ad?"

"Molly, I hate to break this to you, but a personal ad in the *Payne Sentinel* isn't exactly national news."

"I know that. You're the one who insisted we put the personals feature in. It wasn't my idea."

He accepted that gracefully. "Actually, she called because she read in some tabloid that Taylor was planning a birthday party."

"Oh." Molly's hands came up to cradle his face. "I'm sorry," she said softly, her thumbs brushing his ears and sending a lick of fire through his bloodstream.

"It wouldn't have been so infuriating if she'd just called to let me know that Taylor got the date wrong."

"Did she?"

"Beats me," he said. Bitterly, Sam remembered Tuesday's conversation with his mother. She'd sounded angry, as if he'd somehow betrayed her by adapting to life as a Reed. "She's out of money. It seems Edward's settlement didn't last as long as she thought it would."

"Oh." Molly's slid her fingers to his neck where she kneaded the tight muscles. "She asked you for money?"

Again, Sam shook his head. "You know, even that wouldn't have been so bad."

Her eyebrows drew together slightly. "Just tell me, Sam."

He placed his hands on her hips and edged her closer to him. Somehow, her warmth warded off the chill that had settled on him. "She tried to blackmail me."

He sounded so defeated, Molly felt her indignation swell. "Blackmail! What on earth for?"

"It's ironic really." His hands tightened on her hips. "If I don't pay her what she wants before Taylor's party, she plans to tell the tabloids that she lied seventeen years ago and that I'm not really Edward Reed's son.''

"Oh, Sam."

"The hell of it is she's finally telling the truth. She never did have an affair with Edward."

"Then why—"

"Did she claim she did? For the money."

"No. Why did he—"

"Beats the hell out of me," Sam confessed.

Molly exhaled a long, slow breath, and brought one hand around to stroke his cheek. "I'm sorry, Sam."

"So," he went on, "I'm stuck with two choices. I can tell her to go to hell, knowing full well she'll approach the media."

"No one will believe her. No one's going to believe Edward adopted you if he didn't think you were really his."

He shrugged. "It'll be messy and embarrassing and a hell of a nuisance."

"What about Ben and Taylor? How are they going to take this?"

"I doubt they'd care. Actually, Taylor would probably relish the attention from the tabloids. As far as the money's concerned…" He shrugged. "I never took Edward's money anyway. I forced Ben to pump my share of the inheritance back into the business."

"I see."

"But I don't like spectacles, Molly."

She nodded thoughtfully. "I know."

He wasn't sure he wanted to continue. Molly prodded him. "You're angry at her. For what it's worth, I think you have every right to be."

"Hell, yes, I'm angry. God, doesn't the woman understand that I'd have given her the money?"

"People like that only know one way of surviving," Molly said gently. "If manipulation doesn't work, they have no other recourse." She ran a finger along the line of his upper lip. "It's sad."

"It's infuriating."

"And mean," Molly added. "I don't like mean people."

Sam took a moment to relish her fingers traveling the planes of his face. His eyes drifted shut and he whispered her name.

Molly traced one eyebrow, then the other. "Sam?"

"Hmm?"

"That's not the worst part, is it?"

He met her gaze again. She was watching him with an expression that wrenched his heart. "I don't know who I am." He surprised himself with the admission. He hadn't admitted what had made him so angry about the events of the past few days. Though he'd never felt he truly belonged to the Reeds, he'd also never doubted where he'd come from. Now, his mother had changed even that.

"I understand."

"How could you possibly understand, Molly? I spent my afternoon with your family. I've seen how you are together."

With a smile full of womanly wisdom, she said, "You were very charming." She stroked his earlobe as she spoke.

"And having had the advantage of a family like

the Flynns all your life, how in the hell can you tell me you know how I feel?''

''Because,'' she said, sliding both her hands to his nape where she urged him closer. ''I'm adopted.''

Sam's mouth fell open in shock. Molly took advantage of his surprise and kissed him. Her lips were warm and full and sweet, and Sam suddenly felt bombarded with sensation. He wanted to press her for details, demand an explanation. But he was slowly losing his train of thought to the intoxicating sensation of Molly's kiss.

She tasted like hot chocolate and melted marshmallows, and he'd waited too long and wanted her too much. Sam groaned softly as she slid her tongue along his lower lip and purred. There was no other possible definition for that sound. It nearly undid him. Sam slid one hand to her back and pressed her to his chest. ''Molly,'' he murmured against her lips. ''Molly, what—''

She shook her head, leaned into him and deepened the kiss. ''Later, Sam,'' she muttered against his lips. ''Ask me later.''

When her fingertips dipped into the whorl of his ears, Sam felt it all the way to his toes. He pulled his mouth from hers and ground out, ''But you—''

She slid her forefinger along the crease of his lips. ''Not now. Just kiss me.''

Sam did. Hard and thoroughly. Lord, he thought, could he die from too much sensation? He reached for a shred of self-control, not sure Molly knew what she was toying with. He wouldn't be able to hold back much longer. He groaned when she raked her

## Chapter Nine

Molly stretched beneath the sheet and winced at a slight twinge in her lower body. The reminder had her rolling to her side to find a sleeping Sam, his arm slung above his head, his face relaxed, his pose decadent. Molly squinted at the clock on her nightstand. It was just after four. Sam had made love to her twice. The first time had been hot and fast and needy, with hurriedly removed clothes and hasty touching. It had been driven, hungry, too long in the making, Molly realized, not to be like an inferno.

Despite Sam's urging that she let him take her to bed, Molly hadn't wanted a chance to change her mind. She'd known that—the first time, anyway—she'd need to be swept away.

Sam, she realized now, was quite a sweep-awayer. He had plundering skills that would put a pirate to shame. When she'd countered his suggestion that they move away from the counter with a tight squeeze of her thighs around his waist, he hadn't needed another hint. Sam had lifted her from the counter, taken two long strides toward a chair, and proceeded to make her see stars underneath the soft glow of the fan light.

fingertips over his nipples. The fabric of his shirt seemed to amplify rather than dampen the impact of the caress. Sam raised his head, cradled her face in both his hands, and looked deeply into her eyes. "I want you, Molly. Tell me you want this, too." He remembered her lecture that morning and the way she'd tried hard to convince him that she wanted to keep her distance. Her breathing was slightly ragged as she swayed toward him. Sam squeezed her tight. "Tell me," he ordered.

Her eyes drifted shut and she tipped her mouth toward his. "Take me to bed, Sam," she said softly.

True to his word, Sam didn't wait for a second invitation.

Molly wondered, irreverently, if he had splinters in his butt from her antique oak kitchen chairs.

Their lovemaking had been wonderful and mind-numbing and inspiring and overwhelming—like an afternoon thunderstorm that crests the horizon and overtakes the sky with power and force.

But the second time, the time he'd laid her gently on her bed and proceeded to explore every one of her secret places, *that* had been the point where Molly's heart slipped slowly and irrevocably into his keeping. He'd lavished attention on her. He'd praised her skin and its texture, her hair and its color, her body and its softness. With dark whispers and lush words, Sam had made her feel like the sexiest and most beautiful woman alive. When he entered her that second time, Molly had felt things she'd never before experienced. That time, he not only showed her the stars, he took her to them.

Now, in the dim light, she studied his face and remembered the haunted look she'd seen there when he told her about his mother. Gently, Molly brushed a lock of hair from his forehead. Sam stirred and muttered something in his sleep. Whether he was ready to admit it or not, he had felt stricken and set adrift by his mother's revelation. Molly knew the feeling. As a child, she'd wrestled with it herself. There was something frightening about not knowing where you'd come from and who you belonged to. She'd been an adolescent before she finally realized that the family you pick, or the family that picks you, is some-times far better than the one you could get stuck with if nature had its way.

Molly wrapped an arm around his waist and laid

her head on his chest. She understood now why she'd felt so drawn to him. That look in his eyes wasn't just a lonely cry for help. It exactly mirrored what she used to see in her own.

"TELL ME," Sam said three hours later as he swept a hand over her bare hip. "Tell me now?"

Molly didn't pretend not to understand. She'd risen early, made them breakfast and served it to Sam in bed. He'd been watching her warily ever since she crawled back into bed wearing her cow-print pajamas. He wasn't going to wait any longer for an explanation of what she'd told him last night.

Molly took a long sip of her coffee. "I was about three when my birth mother abandoned me at the Payne hospital. Dad was there visiting a friend from work when he overheard the nurses talking about me." She smiled as she recalled the way her parents told this story. "According to Dad, he'd been telling Mama he wanted another daughter. According to Mama, she'd been telling him he'd have to get another wife if he wanted any more babies."

Sam studied her through narrowed eyes. "Your father brought you home from the hospital?"

Molly laughed. "Lord, no, Sam, it's not quite that easy. Adopting a child isn't like adopting a puppy, you know. There are papers and legal documents and security checks, and all kinds of stuff. Dad pulled a couple of strings and got Child Services to agree to let them be my foster parents until everything was sorted out. The police spent several months trying to find my birth mother, and Dad spent those months convincing Mama that whether I was born a Flynn or not, I looked and acted enough like one that I should be one.''

''How did your sisters feel?'' He placed his hand on the flat of her stomach.

''I don't remember much about it. They say it was a little strained at first. It was a big change and all that.'' Molly covered his hand with hers. ''I was one more person to share Mama and Dad's attention, and my sisters didn't like it. Not to mention the fact that I was costing a lot of money.''

Sam frowned. ''Money?''

''Legal bills. And hospital bills. Family health insurance doesn't cover expenses for a child you bring home from the hospital because nobody else wanted her.'' She stroked the back of his hand. ''It wasn't easy, but Dad and Mama were determined. It took a couple of years before everything was final.''

''And you became a Flynn.''

She grinned at him. ''We had a ceremony. Flynns are big on ceremonies.''

''I noticed that.''

''My sisters inducted me into the family.''

''What's involved in a Flynn family induction?'' he asked.

''Well, I can't tell you all of it. It's a secret ritual. Outsiders only get the facts when they marry in—or, um, opt in, I guess, like I did.''

''There's a ritual?'' He sounded nervous.

''My sisters' husbands all survived it unscathed. I assure you, it's not that bad.''

''I see.'' Sam leaned back against the pillows. ''And from that day forward, you felt like a Flynn.''

''Well, no, not really,'' Molly confessed. Those

had been confusing times for her, difficult times. Times when she'd wondered what had made her birth mother decide to leave her behind in a hospital. "It took me awhile. I worried a lot while growing up that if I screwed up too bad, they'd send me back." She gave him a dry look. "I'm sure this will come as a complete shock to you, but I'm pretty good at screwing up."

He rolled his eyes. "You don't say."

"I was stressed about it for a long time."

"What changed your mind?"

"The day I totaled Dad's new car. He'd had it a week. I was driving to school to pick up Colleen. I had friends in the car even though I wasn't supposed to. I got distracted and went off the road. Thank God nobody was seriously hurt. The car, though…" She shrugged. "Let's just say there's a reason I drive a twenty-year-old Beetle."

"I've seen you drive," he told her. "I know why."

Molly gave him a playful swat. "I figured for sure that the car was going to be the last straw. I mean, with your own kids, you sort of have this built-in life contract thing, but when the kids are somebody else's—well, I wasn't sure the same rules applied."

"You were what, sixteen, by then?"

"A few days over sixteen. I'd had my license less than a week."

He tilted his head. "You were still afraid of being sent away eleven *years* after your parents adopted you?"

"It wasn't their fault, Sam. I just couldn't get over the fact that my birth mother dropped me off at a hospital and never, to my knowledge, even tried to find out if I was okay.''

He scrubbed at his day's growth of whiskers. Molly found it unbearably sexy to hear the rough sound against his hand. ''I can understand that,'' he told her.

She forged ahead. ''Wrecking the car was a watershed event. I figured out that unconditional love doesn't mean you never get angry—Dad was plenty angry. It just means you don't give up. Not ever. I found an incredible sense of security in knowing that when my family took me in and made me a Flynn, as far as they were concerned, the contract was binding. No backing out. No escape clause. No money-back guarantee.''

''I'm sure you did.''

Molly squeezed his hand. ''Taylor and Ben feel that way about you, Sam.''

He gave her a shrewd look. ''What makes you say that?''

''It's the way they talk *to* you, the way they talk *about* you. It's family. I happen to be an expert on the subject of family. I know one when I see one.''

''Is this the part where I'm supposed to tell you how I'm feeling about all this?''

''No. I don't need to know how you feel.''

He rolled his head to the side with an incredulous look. ''You're kidding.''

''No,'' she assured him.

''Women always want to know how men feel.''

''That's a disgusting generalization, Sam. I gave you more credit than that.''

''In my experience,'' he clarified, ''women always want to know how men feel.''

Molly clucked her tongue. "Then it's your fault for getting involved with crummy women."

Sam searched her face. Molly wondered if he found what he was looking for. "Then why did you tell me that story?" he finally asked.

She set her mug on the nightstand, cleared the breakfast tray and turned to him. "Because. I wanted you to know how I feel." Her fingers went to the buttons of her pajama top.

He definitely looked interested. "Oh?"

"Mm-hmm." She flicked open the top two buttons.

Sam started working at the bottom buttons. "I feel," Molly said, "that I have an article to write today with a four o'clock deadline, and that if I want to make love to you again, we'd better get to it."

Sam stared at her a moment, astonished, then started to laugh. "Molly—"

She slipped out of the pajama top. "Come on, Sam. I realize the cow pajamas may not have put you in the—" She squealed when he deftly rolled to his side and slid her beneath him in a move of seamless and effortless grace.

"It might surprise you to learn, Ms. Flynn," he said, his lips pressed to her ear, "that I find cow-print pajamas unbearably sexy."

"Sam—"

He nipped the spot beneath her ear, making her moan. "It's true," he whispered. "I've been aching for you since you plopped that breakfast tray on my lap."

Molly wound her arms around his neck. "Oh,

good," she said. "And here I was worried that I wouldn't have time to seduce you before I had to get to my story."

"BECAUSE, TAYLOR," Sam told his sister patiently on the phone later that afternoon, "I haven't asked the woman to marry me." Having met Molly and the Flynns at the duck races, Taylor had wasted no time pressing forward with her usual agenda. She'd called Sam to ensure that Molly was coming to his party. He'd assured her she was. She also wanted to know whether she could begin discussing Sam's wedding plans. He'd assured her she could not.

Sam had left Molly's house that morning before noon, knowing she had a deadline to meet and that there'd be four days of work in his inbox. Once at the office he'd been unable to concentrate. In fact, he'd restrained himself from calling her that afternoon. He felt foolish and more than a little unsettled that his apparently unrelenting hunger for her had not been assuaged during the night—or this morning.

Thoughts of the morning had a predictable effect on him. He'd never known flannel pajamas could be so sexy. Of course, it probably wasn't the flannel pajamas as much as what was *under* the pajamas. After weeks of speculating about Molly's lingerie, Sam had been gratified to learn that he still had keen instincts. Yesterday, under her sweatshirt and jeans, she'd worn a lemon-yellow bra and panty set to the duck races. Yellow, he guessed, for ducks. On some women, the color might have looked harsh, but on Molly the warm hue did something wonderful and unpredictable to her skin. This morning, as the cow-print pajamas were coming off, Sam had discovered a pair of coral lace panties that accented her freckles and her rich red hair. His head had spun.

He wondered if Molly knew how this newfound knowledge would torture him in the days ahead. How would he stand sitting across from her in a meeting knowing—

"Sam—" Taylor insisted. "Sam, are you still there?"

Sam shut his eyes in frustration. He'd snatched up the phone before the second ring, hopeful that Molly was calling to tell him she'd finished her article on the duck races. He had not been in the mood for Taylor's well-intentioned meddling. "Yeah," he told her as he shoved aside a stack of financial reports. "I'm here."

"I like her," Taylor said. "I like her *a lot.*"

"You like the fact that you think she got the better of me with that ad."

"It didn't hurt," his sister admitted. "But it's more than that. She's—real. I never really thought that about Pamela."

Sam didn't want to think about Pamela. Somehow, the idea of comparing Molly to Pamela left a bad taste in his mouth. "Molly and Pamela don't have much in common," he agreed.

"Except for you," Taylor pointed out. "They both attracted you."

Not really, Sam thought wearily. Pamela had been convenient and appropriate—precisely the kind of woman a Reed should marry. After Ben's very public engagement, Sam had felt drawn to Pamela's suitability. Too bad, he thought bitterly, he'd nearly missed her more obvious flaws. "Look," he told his sister, "I lost a lot of time last week. I don't mean to rush you, but—"

"Speaking of last week," his sister interrupted. "Have you heard from Rhea again?"

"No," Sam said flatly. He had not spoken to his mother since their heated discussion on Friday afternoon.

"Did you decide what you're going to do?"

"Not yet." Fresh in his mind was the healing memory of Molly's arms around his shoulders and her legs around his waist and of the very real sense that he finally belonged somewhere. Rhea's threats had faded somewhat in the face of making love to Molly Flynn. Another miracle, Sam mused, to add to his list of things to ponder later.

"You want my opinion?" Taylor asked.

"Aren't you going to give it to me whether I want it or not?"

"Probably."

He sighed. "Then go ahead."

"I think you should tell her to stick it."

Sam thought that over. "You know what'll happen, Taylor."

"She'll call the tabloids. Big deal. Don't you remember last month when they announced that soap star was the child of alien parents? Nobody takes that stuff seriously, Sam."

"I don't know about you, but I'd still rather avoid having to tromp through the mud."

"I know, but if you buy her off, she'll come back again. Whatever Daddy gave her obviously didn't do the trick."

Sam mentally squashed his frustration. He

couldn't—nor did he want—to explain to his sister why his mother's extortion attempt was taking such a toll on him. Briefly, he remembered Molly telling him about her experience with the Flynns. What Molly didn't understand was that she'd had the advantage of a family that had allowed her to assimilate. Sam hadn't. "You may be right," he told Taylor, hoping to head off another lecture.

Taylor's sigh was exasperated. "Well, whatever you do, please make sure you discuss it with me and Ben first. You know we're on your side, Sam."

"Sure," he said noncommittally.

"And you're bringing Molly to the party?" Taylor prompted.

"Yes. I'm bringing her to the party."

"You sound worried," she said. "What have you got to be worried about?"

"You know how I feel about this party."

"Oh, pooh, Sam. You're thrilled and you know it."

He didn't argue. He'd given up weeks ago. "I'm just not sure Molly will enjoy herself."

"Not enjoy—you think she's going to be put off by us when we're all together, don't you?"

"Taylor," he said with strained patience, "when have you ever known me to worry about something like that?"

"You *are* worried. Why?"

When he didn't respond, Taylor continued, "I mean, she's already met Mother and Aunt Margaret. That went all right, didn't it?"

"As well as could be expected, I guess."

"I talked to Mother before the duck races. She said

Margaret found Molly charming. Mother seemed to like her, too.''

"In case you haven't noticed, I'm not really concerned about what the Reeds think of the women in my life.''

"I know, I know. It's got more to do with her than it has with us.''

"Not all of you,'' Sam conceded.

"Sam,'' his sister said thoughtfully, "you're really serious about her, aren't you?''

"Don't read anything into this,'' he warned.

"You've never really cared before whether they met your family or not.''

"Molly's different.''

"I'll say.''

"She's not used to the kind of environment we live in, Taylor. Payne may only be an hour and a half from Boston, but in some respects, it's a world away.''

"I know that, but I have it on very good authority, Sam, that most people consider Reed males to be very good catches. Molly may be from a small town, but she's in publishing, for God's sake. She's got to know who we are.''

"Oh, she knows.''

"Then I can't imagine that she'll be put off by meeting your family.''

"She won't be put off,'' he assured his sister. Molly struck him as the kind of woman who was comfortable just about anywhere. She liked herself. She was proud of her life and her family and it showed. Sam, who had come by his own personal acceptance through a tougher-than-usual route, admired her for that. He couldn't really explain his reluctance. It had nothing to do with Molly's ability to adapt, and much more to do with what she might think of him when it was over.

Not wanting to contemplate the implications of that, Sam abruptly closed the subject. "I've already told you she's planning on coming," he said to his sister. "That'll have to be enough."

His remark seemed to appease her. "That's fair enough."

"Thank God."

Taylor laughed. "Oh, don't be so sour," she chided him. "You know I wouldn't nag if I didn't care about you."

"You're meddling, Taylor."

"Of *course* I'm meddling, Sam. It's what I do."

"And you excel at it," he said. "Just like everything else."

"If I *excelled* at it, darling, I'd have managed to get both my older brothers married years ago."

"Point well taken," Sam said smoothly. "If there's nothing else—"

"There's one more thing. Amy and I talked on the ride back yesterday about calling Molly this week and seeing if we could get together for a girl's day. I think we'd all enjoy the chance to get to know one another a little."

"Taylor—"

"I need her number," his sister broke in. "Or should I just wait and call her at the office tomorrow?"

Sam had a strong suspicion that Molly's idea of girl stuff would not entail the day at the spa he was certain his sister had in mind. Molly was not the primping type. But he'd let her cross that bridge with his sister. "She's on deadline today," he explained. "I'd try her tomorrow."

"You think she'll go?"

"No," he said. "She's not going to take a day off to go shopping. She's married to the newspaper."

Taylor laughed. "For now she is."

"What do you mean 'for now?'"

"If I have my way, Sam, it won't be long before she's married to *you.*"


"WHAT ABOUT THIS ONE?" Colleen held up a dress for Molly's inspection.

Molly wrinkled her nose. "Bad cut." It was Wednesday afternoon. Molly had met her sister for lunch every day that week in search of a dress for Sam's party. She couldn't decide whether she felt guiltier about wasting the time shopping, or about the relentless need she felt to find a dress. In her life, Molly couldn't remember worrying about clothes except for her sister Eileen's wedding. Eileen had chosen lime-green bridesmaid dresses. Everyone worried about the clothes at Eileen's wedding.

Colleen returned the dress to the rack and held up another. "You're never this picky," she pointed out.

Molly looked at the green dress. "Bad—everything." Frustrated, she flipped through another rack of clothes. She had a deadline looming on the first installment of her transportation story. Why couldn't this shopping business be as easy for her as other—

Colleen showed Molly yet another choice. "This?"

The dress had ruffles. Molly hadn't worn ruffles

since first grade. She glared at Colleen. "What *are* you thinking?"

"Okay, okay. I quit. We're not going to find whatever it is you're looking for here."

Or probably anywhere, Molly thought glumly. Sighing, she glanced quickly at her watch. "I've got to go back to the office anyway. I've got a four o'clock deadline."

"Okay. Same time tomorrow?"

"The party's Friday."

"I told you, I have that amber dress you can borrow. You've always liked it."

"On you. I've always liked it on you."

"What's wrong with the brown one you bought a couple of years ago?"

"I wear it to funerals," Molly said. "It's a funeral dress."

"That doesn't mean—"

"I'm not wearing a funeral dress to Sam's birthday party."

Colleen gave her a shrewd look. "I don't suppose it's occurred to you—"

"That I'm making too big a deal of this? Yes, as a matter of fact it has."

Colleen blinked. "Oh."

"Surprised?"

Her sister nodded as they walked toward the door. "In my experience, you're usually the last to know when you're about to wade in too deep."

Molly pushed open the glass door and emerged onto the busy sidewalk. The wind had picked up, so she wrapped her fleece jacket around her. "You think I'm in too deep with Sam?" Colleen hesitated.

"What?" Molly pressed her. "You were going to say something."

"Well, it's just that…"

Molly stopped walking. "I want to know what you were going to say."

Colleen took a careful breath. "You seem serious, Mol. Really serious."

Molly contemplated that. Considering Sam had spent every night since Sunday in her bed; considering that they were lovers and intimate friends; considering that she was beginning to picture what her life would be like when he was no longer in it; she'd have to say that yes, she was fairly serious. "Why do you say that?" she hedged.

"Are you sleeping with him?"

"You've never asked me that before."

Colleen shrugged and began walking up the sidewalk again. "It never seemed relevant before. The men you dated—I didn't think you'd ever actually fall in love with them."

"Colleen—"

"I'm serious. They were okay guys, don't get me wrong, but you weren't the type to settle for an okay guy. Me, I'm the kind of woman who falls for a man like Todd. He's stable, he's predictable—and don't you dare say he's boring."

"I don't think Todd is boring," Molly objected.

"You did when I first started dating him."

"He grew on me."

"Which is my point," her sister said. "Sam—he's not in the same league."

"And you think he's out of mine."

"Don't get defensive. I'm just worried." Colleen

sighed, and her breath formed a plume of mist in the crisp fall air. "I don't want you to get hurt."

"You sound like Eileen."

"I'm your sister. I know you. I love you."

"And you think Sam's going to hurt me."

"I think that Sam's going to outgrow Payne in another couple of months. You told me yourself that the paper was showing signs of improvement."

Molly had avoided thinking about this for many reasons. "We have a very long way to go before we're back on track. Years, maybe, before the *Sentinel* fully recovers."

"How much of that journey will Sam have to be here for?"

"I don't know."

"Not much? Some? A lot? Come on, you can't tell me you haven't thought about it."

"I'm trying not to," Molly told her sister. They reached the corner across the street from the *Sentinel.* Molly shoved her hands into her jacket pockets to ward off the chill. "Look, Colleen, I appreciate your concern—"

Her sister placed a hand on her arm. "I'm not meddling," she told Molly. "I just want you to know I think you're in love with Sam. I don't want him to break your heart, that's all."

"And you think it's inevitable."

"He doesn't strike me as the kind of man who gives his heart away. And you're not the kind of woman who settles for less. When it comes right down to it, Molly, you aren't going to accept any less from him than a complete surrender. I just don't think he's the type to give it to you."

Molly studied her sister. "I'll be all right," she said softly. "I couldn't have lived with myself if I hadn't—" From the corner of her eye, something near the *Sentinel* entrance caught her attention. She glanced across the street and studied the two black sedans that had rolled to a stop in front of the building. "I've got to go, Colleen. All right?"

Her sister followed her gaze to the two vehicles. "Trouble?"

"I don't know." Molly jabbed the button on the light post that activated the crosswalk. "I'm going to find out."

"Same time tomorrow?" her sister asked as the light changed.

Molly nodded. "Same time tomorrow."

# Chapter Ten

Sam gave Molly a cautioning look as she entered his office ten minutes later. "Molly. Glad you could join us."

She glanced at the four men seated across from him. "I just got your message. Sorry if I'm late."

The four men had risen. Sam introduced them as officials from the Boston Department of Transportation and the Election Commission. "We're not the only ones looking into the mayor's transportation project," Sam explained. "Have a seat, Molly."

She raised an eyebrow, but took the remaining empty chair. "What's going on?"

One of the election officials handed Molly a bound report. "As you probably know, the governor launched a major initiative last year to clean up the election process in our state. We've successfully prosecuted fifteen cases, and have twice that many under investigation."

Molly nodded as she leafed through the report. The most publicized case had been a federal prosecution against a Massachusetts congressman for bribery. "I covered the congressional case for the *Sentinel*."

"We're not just looking at federal officials," the other election official told her. "The governor has asked us to examine local elections as well."

Molly glanced at Sam. "Cobell?"

"The Department of Transportation," Sam said, indicating the other two men, "has some concerns about the bidding process for the hub."

"They should," she responded. "I've done the research." In her investigation she'd discovered evidence of everything from fraudulent environmental reports to suppressed zoning laws and possible election tampering in the mayoral race. She'd assumed that no one had been paying very close attention, or Cobell couldn't have gotten away with so much.

"We're extremely interested in your research, Ms. Flynn," the youngest of the four men said. Sam had introduced him as Ronnie Teasdale, an environmental engineer for the transportation department. "We'd like the chance to compare it to our own."

"Sure," Molly told them. "I'm filing a major story this afternoon. It'll run Friday as the teaser for our front-page edition on Saturday. In case you don't know, small-town papers have a greater circulation on Saturdays." She shrugged. "It comes as a surprise to a lot of people, but yard-sale shoppers also read the front-page news. You can have a copy of everything I've got after I'm done writing the piece."

One of the election officials coughed. Ronnie Teasdale gave her a grave look. "That's why we're here, Ms. Flynn. We came to persuade you and Mr. Reed that running the transportation piece right now may not be in the best interests of our investigation."

Molly stared at him. "It's in the best interests of the people of Payne."

"Not if it hinders us from exposing further corruption," Teasdale argued.

Molly glanced at Sam. "What do you think about this?"

Sam steepled his fingers beneath his chin and gave her a grave look. "That's why I asked you to join us."

The election official Sam had introduced as Martin Deslin said, "Mr. Reed felt you should be consulted before a final decision was made."

Molly tossed the report onto Sam's desk. "I can't believe you're asking me not to report on what we've learned."

"Not to report it *now*," Teasdale countered.

Her temper rose another notch. "Do you expect me to believe that if the *Payne Sentinel* were the *Boston Globe,* you'd even be having this conversation?"

"It might surprise you to learn," Deslin said, "that we have these kinds of conversations with editors at the *Globe* all the time."

"Do they do any good?" Molly asked. The four men had the grace to look uncomfortable. "I didn't think so." She met Sam's eyes. "I hope you told them it's out of the question. We're supposed to break the first part of the story on Friday."

"I told them we might consider waiting to run your teaser until the Monday evening edition."

Her mouth dropped open. "Sam—"

"We asked for two weeks," Teasdale said.

Sam nodded. "I told them that was out of the question."

Molly leaped to her feet and leaned over Sam's desk. "Don't you know what this is? They're trying to coerce us into letting them break the story first. It's politics. The governor's office doesn't want the public to think we discovered what was going on before they did."

His expression remained inscrutable. "I know exactly what's going on," he assured her. "And I'm interested in the public good."

"You're supposed to be interested in the good of the *Payne Sentinel*."

"The two don't necessarily have to be in conflict."

"Sam—"

He met her gaze and held it for a long, breathless second. "You have to trust me, Molly."

He'd trapped her neatly, she realized. His mind was already made up, and the ruse of letting her in on the decision actually had no bearing on its outcome. Molly straightened slowly and turned to face the four men. "Well then, I guess your trip from Boston was time well spent. It looks like we won't be breaking the story before you schedule a press conference."

Ronnie Teasdale was pulling on his tie. "Er, there is the small matter of your research—"

Molly glared at him. "Do your own damned research," she said, and stalked out of the office.

She was muttering under her breath, tossing personal items into a box when Sam and the four men swept through the main floor of the *Sentinel*. She'd been fending off her colleagues' questions since she'd stormed out of the elevator. Around her, activity had continued at its usual breakneck pace, except for the occasional curious glance. When the large glass doors swished shut behind the four visitors and Sam turned to face her, his expression was tense and frustrated, and the room fell suddenly silent.

Cindy Freesdon gasped out loud as Sam took several measured strides toward Molly's desk. "I'd like to see you upstairs," he said through clenched teeth.

Molly fingered the clay pencil cup—another Christmas present from her artistically inclined nieces—and thought that over. "No," she said finally. "Whatever you have to say to me, you can say it here."

Every eye in the newsroom was trained on them. Sam's gaze narrowed. "Molly—"

She looked around. "We're like a family, here, Sam. I'm not sure you ever really got that."

He hesitated. "I'd rather not—"

"I'm sure you wouldn't." Molly wrapped the pencil cup in some tissues and stuffed it into the box. "But I would. I think they have a right to know what's going on."

"Nothing," he said, his voice a low warning, "is going on."

"Sure it is. You just sold us out so you wouldn't have to tick off your family's friends in the governor's office."

She was fairly certain she saw rage flicker in his gaze. "It didn't have a damned thing to do with that."

"Didn't it?" Molly placed her hands on her hips. "You forget, Sam. I was there when you got that call last night from Mark Slenton. Don't you think I know he's the governor's press secretary?"

"I didn't try to hide it from you."

"You also didn't bother to tell me what the call

was about. Personal business, you said. He's a friend of the Reeds.''

''He is.''

''And because he's a friend of the Reeds, he called in a favor. The governor doesn't want to be trumped by a small-town paper. You agreed to give Slenton time to put his own spin on this story.''

By now, the editorial staff had begun forming a semicircle around her desk. They were watching Sam with a mix of fascination, anxiety and anger.

''You don't know what you're talking about,'' Sam said quietly. ''I really wish you'd come upstairs with me.''

''No.'' She scooped up another stack of personal papers and threw them in the box. ''That's the whole problem. You haven't been telling me the whole story, and I haven't been telling you the whole story.'' She looked around at the other occupants of the room. ''And Sam and I haven't been honest with you, either.'' Molly took a deep breath. ''Before I ran that personal ad, Sam and I hadn't even had a private conversation.'' She paused to let that sink in.

''Molly—'' Sam warned.

She held up a hand, but didn't look at him. ''It's true. I know you've all assumed from what's been going on here the last couple of weeks, that things were okay between us. That was Sam's idea.'' Behind her, she heard Sam swear. She ignored him. ''And I agreed to it because I owed him that much. He should have fired me for running that ad. It was juvenile and irresponsible, and it caused him considerable embarrassment. When he asked me if I would stay on here at the *Sentinel* and allow all of you to think we'd had some kind of lover's quarrel, I agreed." Molly shoved her hands in the back pockets of her jeans. "I'm sorry. We deceived you. It was unfair."

Cindy took a step forward. "Nobody thinks—"

"It was," Molly insisted. "You people have been my friends for years. But instead of simply facing the consequences of a stupid mistake, I let everything get out of control." She shook her head. "Now the stakes are too high. What it comes down to is this: We have a chance to break the biggest story this paper has ever known in Saturday's edition." No one in the newsroom was unaware of the implications of the transportation story she'd been working on since last Monday. At Friday's editorial meeting, although Sam was still in Boston, he'd relayed his instructions to leave space for a three-page spread in the Saturday morning edition.

Molly went on. "But the governor's office has asked us to sit on it so *they* can break the story first."

"There are political reasons," Sam said. "They think Cobell is involved in election fraud."

Molly shot him a quelling look. "I was planning to cover that in the piece. They could have taken it from there."

"It's a good compromise," he insisted.

"That's just it," she said angrily. "It's a compromise. That's the difference between you and me. I take what we do here seriously. I don't think we should have to compromise just because we're a small-town paper. If the governor's that interested in this story, he can call and give me a quote for it." She could feel the momentum in the room shifting in her direction. Sam was watching her warily.

"You don't understand—"

"That's where you're wrong. I'm the one who gets it. I'm the one who sees that no matter what you said about wanting to maintain the integrity and character of the *Sentinel,* when it comes right down to it, your Reed name and your Reed connections got in your way. The governor called, and you couldn't turn him down. Well, you know what, Sam," she scooped up her box, "that's the biggest difference between you and Carl. Carl would have told the governor to shove it." She shouldered past Sam and exited the large glass doors without looking back.

THURSDAY'S WEATHER WAS dreary and wet, and the dark skies perfectly matched Sam's mood. He was bringing the *Sentinel*'s new editorial director up to speed on some long-range plans he'd discussed with Carl. Sam had decided last night that the time had come for him to play a lesser role at the paper. He could still give directions from his Boston office, and with the help of his fax machine, high-speed internet access and laptop, from just about anywhere in the world. After yesterday's fiasco in the newsroom, the only hope he had of extricating himself from the situation with any dignity was to leave the *Sentinel* in other hands.

He'd tried calling Molly three times yesterday. Either she wasn't home or she wasn't taking his calls. Twice last night he'd stopped himself from going to her house and demanding that she talk to him. He couldn't decide whether he was more furious that she'd jumped to conclusions or that she'd been partially right.

When he'd arrived at the *Sentinel* that morning, there had been a pall over the newsroom. Without commenting, Sam had dropped his key to Molly's brownstone onto her nearly empty desk. The sound of the key plinking on the laminated desktop had seemed startlingly loud in the nearly silent room where everyone was watching him. This was twice in as many weeks, Sam had thought moodily as he stalked toward the elevator, that Molly had turned his life into a spectacle.

His assistant had been tiptoeing around him all day. He'd managed to avoid his sister's calls twice, but figured he couldn't put her off much longer. A brief conversation with Ben had confirmed what Sam already knew: that Ben was eager to have him back in Boston on bigger projects than the *Sentinel*. Sam couldn't explain why he didn't find the idea as tantalizing as he should. Ben had informed him there was still work to do in London, and that they were considering a major buyout in the Midwest. Sam usually enjoyed the challenge and pace of the negotiations, but today the burden seemed unnaturally heavy.

"Er, Mr. Reed—"

The editorial director was looking at him curiously. Belatedly, Sam realized he'd been staring out the window. "Sorry, Greg. My mind's not on this, I guess."

Greg Jessen, a talented writer and outstanding editor Sam had discovered languishing in the *Sentinel*'s editorial department, was looking at him curiously. "I, um, wasn't at work yesterday."

"I heard," Sam told him. "Your daughter's school play. How was it?"

''Fine, fine. Shakespeare survived the third grade at Payne Elementary.''

''Glad to hear it.''

''I heard, though,'' Greg said. ''About Molly.''

Sam's lips twisted into a slight grimace. ''I imagine everyone's heard.''

''I hope that's not the reason—''

''That I'm leaving?'' Sam interrupted. ''I assure you. Reed Enterprises has plenty of projects demanding my attention.''

Greg took the change of subject gracefully. ''Well, good. I would hate to think—''

''And *you're* more than ready to take charge.'' Sam reached for a stack of reports. ''I wouldn't ask you to step into this role if you weren't.'' He handed the stack to Greg. ''Let's get started.''

MOLLY WAS AN EXPERT at wallowing. She'd made an art of it. True wallowing required sad old movies, lots of tissues, several pints of gourmet chocolate ice cream, comfortable flannel pajamas and serious eye-reddening, nose-running sobs.

She was more than twenty-four hours into full wallow when she heard a knock at her door. She glanced at the clock. It was nearly three on Thursday afternoon. She'd switched on her answering machine and taken few calls. When she'd phoned her sister to say she couldn't make their lunch date, Colleen had begged to come over. Molly had refused.

Colleen knew her sister well. She understood that the time alone was crucial to Molly's healing. She promised to wait until Friday, but if Molly hadn't emerged by then from her self-imposed cocoon, Colleen would come for her.

The knock sounded again, more insistently. Molly had a sinking feeling that it might be Sam. He'd tried to call, but she'd turned down the volume on the answering machine so she couldn't hear his message. She'd ignored his pages and calls to her cell phone as well.

The knocking continued. Molly padded reluctantly to the door, not sure whether she hoped or feared she'd find Sam on the other side.

She checked the peephole to find Taylor Reed, looking distressed and worried. Frowning, Molly pulled open the door. Taylor's hand was poised in midair, prepared to knock again. "Oh, Molly," she said. "Thank God!"

Molly frowned again. To her delight and surprise, Molly had come to like Sam's sister. Though she'd spoken to her only once since the day of the duck races, Molly had admitted to herself and to Sam that there was something endearing about Taylor's flamboyant personality. Even today, she was dressed in a tangerine designer jumpsuit with matching hat and sunglasses. On most women, the outfit would have looked garish and comical. Taylor Reed, Molly was learning, was not most women.

"Lord, Molly," Taylor said, staring at her closely. "You look as bad as I feel."

"Thanks," Molly quipped.

Taylor shook her head. "I don't mean it that way. I just mean that when Sam wouldn't take my calls—well, I suspected something like this."

Molly raised an eyebrow and leaned against her door frame. "Like what?"

"Sam screwed up with you, didn't he?"

"You could say that."

"It's a pattern," Taylor assured Molly. "He *always* does this. That's why I had to see you. I—I think you're good for Sam."

"Some people would tell you I'm too good for Sam."

Taylor managed a laugh. "I'm sure they would." She glanced past Molly's shoulder. "Please, may I come in? At least let me try to help you understand."

Molly hesitated, but finally stepped away from the door. Taylor swept into the small foyer with the dignity of the queen of England paying a royal visit. Molly had noticed that Taylor never simply walked— she swept. Annoyed by this observation, Molly led Taylor to her living room. If Taylor found anything untoward about the mound of crumpled tissues and the discarded ice cream containers, she said nothing. Instead, she sat in the overstuffed chair where Sam had fallen asleep the night he'd returned from Boston. "All right," she said as soon as Molly was seated on the sofa, "tell me what he did."

"WHAT THE HELL do you mean you thought she was with me?" Sam demanded of his brother later that night. "I haven't seen her since last week." He'd returned to Boston, his mood sour, with every intention of telling Taylor she'd have to plan on his absence at her party. When he'd been unable to find his sister, he'd gone to see Ben.

Ben looked at him curiously. "She left this afternoon. Said she was heading for Payne."

"Oh, hell," Sam muttered.

His sister-in-law joined her husband at the door of their penthouse apartment. "Honey? Is something wrong?" Her eyes widened when she saw Sam. "Oh, Sam. Hi."

Ben glanced at his wife. "What do you know about Taylor?"

A smile played at the corners of Amy's mouth. "Let me count the ways," she said.

"Today," Ben said. "What do you know about why she's in Payne today?"

"Oh." Amy patted Sam on the arm. "Because Sam screwed up his relationship with Molly."

"Oh, Lord," Ben groaned.

Sam swore.

Amy looked at him with raised eyebrows. "Well, you did, didn't you?" she asked Sam.

Ben wiped a hand over his face. "And naturally, you and Taylor felt you needed to get involved."

"Naturally." She pulled on Sam's arm. "Come on in, Sam. You look terrible."

He hesitated, but Amy insisted. "Come on. There's nothing you can do about it right now. Taylor's trying to fix it for you."

"That gives me great comfort," Sam said.

"Me, too." Ben's expression was pained.

"I wouldn't worry about it if I were you," Amy assured them. "Taylor's actually better at this than either of you think."

"The voice of experience?" her husband asked, his tone indulgent.

"I did end up marrying you, didn't I?" Amy shot back. She headed for the kitchen. "Why don't I make us some tea," she volunteered. "I have a feeling it's going to be a long night."

As she walked down the hall, Sam muttered, "Better make mine a double."

MOLLY HAD A SICK FEELING in the pit of her stomach. She wished she could blame it on the ice cream, but as Taylor's story unfolded, she felt her stomach twisting into knots.

"I'm not going to tell you it was easy," Taylor continued. "When Sam first came to live with us, Ben and I were both angry at our father."

"I'm sure."

"You know, his mother didn't actually have any evidence for her claims."

"Sam told me about it last week."

Taylor leaned back in her chair with a sigh of disgust. "I still don't think he's decided what to do about the woman."

"I told him to blow her off."

"Me, too."

"It would cause a scandal. Sam hates scandals."

"Can you blame him?" Taylor asked. "He's spent most of his life wishing he could disappear. Even though Daddy brought him to live with us, I don't think Sam ever felt like he fit." She tipped her head to one side. "Did he happen to tell you that he never accepted any of Daddy's money?"

"He put it back into the business."

"Yes," Taylor confirmed. "Ben argued with him, but Sam was insistent." She shook her head. "He always resented Daddy for not claiming him sooner—so you can imagine what it did to him when his mother said that Edward wasn't his father.''

"No identity," Molly said.

"If he can't be angry at Edward, he's got no one to blame." Taylor frowned. "That woman is a menace.''

"Sounds like it."

Taylor shifted in the chair. "So that's why I came down here today. Sam needs you, Molly." At Molly's dubious look, Taylor nodded. "He does. The last woman—"

"Pamela?"

Taylor's eyebrows lifted. "He told you about Pamela?''

"He *mentioned* her," Molly clarified.

"I'm not surprised." Taylor studied her manicured fingernails for a moment. "That was a spectacular disaster.''

"I think that's what Sam said."

"Pamela was completely suitable. She was exactly the kind of woman the entire family thought a Reed should marry. I think Sam dated her because Ben's engagement to Amy scared the crud out of him.''

"I read some of the coverage." Molly remembered seeing the tabloids in the grocery store.

"Then you know. Amy's wonderful, and I adore her. She's like the sister I never had, but things were rocky. Ben's *not* the easiest person in the world to get along with—and Lord knows, Sam is worse.''

"I can believe that."

"And frankly, I have to take some of the blame for what happened between Sam and Pamela. I got so caught up in Ben's wedding plans that Sam was probably afraid I'd set my sights on him next.''

''Did you?''

''They are my brothers. I want them to be happy.''

''I can understand that.'' Molly thought about the mixed emotions she'd experienced when her sisters had announced their engagements. She had been thrilled for them yet had experienced a deep sense of loss in knowing that they belonged to someone else.

''Especially Sam,'' Taylor said. ''I've always had a soft spot for Sam.''

''He's like a stray?'' Molly guessed. ''And you can't quite help yourself?''

''Exactly.'' Taylor looked relieved. ''I knew I liked you. You get him, don't you?''

''I think Sam is the kind of man who never completely gives his heart.''

''He's been hurt too often,'' Taylor said. ''Too many people have taken advantage of him.'' She paused. ''Even Pamela. She was very attracted to Sam's family ties and to his money. I think she decided if she couldn't have Ben, Sam was the next best choice.''

''What happened?''

''Sam found out that Pamela's father hoped the relationship would put some much-needed capital into his failing business. Also Pamela wanted Sam's money and his name, and when she found out that he'd dumped his inheritance back into Reed Enterprises—'' Taylor shrugged ''—she lost interest.''

''Ugh.'' Distaste and outrage filled her.

''Don't get me wrong. Sam's done well for himself, but Pamela's father was looking for a major infusion. Sam wasn't going to give it to him, so Pamela left him three days before their wedding.''

"He didn't love her," Molly insisted. She'd known that from the way Sam talked about Pamela.

"No," Taylor agreed. "But she was one more person in his life who had used him. It still hurt."

Molly thought that over. "Like his mother."

"Yes," Taylor agreed. "Like his mother."

Molly sank back in the couch and pulled a cotton blanket around her legs. "So what has all this got to do with me, Taylor?"

"I think you're in love with my brother," Taylor said.

Molly felt her eyes begin to tear again. "It doesn't matter."

"I think it matters a lot."

"Sam and I are too different. There's no way—"

"Molly," Taylor handed Molly a tissue. "Don't you see? It's the fact that you *are* different that makes me think you're Sam's best hope for happiness."

Molly blew her nose inelegantly and shook her head. "It won't work. Not after yesterday." She filled Taylor in on the details of the transportation story and Sam's apparent bargain with the governor's office. "It wasn't the story," Molly insisted. "I was angry about the story, but that wasn't really the point."

"I know."

"It's that he can't see why something like this would be important to me. I can't change who I am. I don't want to change who I am. I love Payne. I love my life here. And I can't be the kind of person who cuts a political deal despite what I know is right."

"I don't think Sam is either," Taylor mused.

"You weren't there." Molly couldn't keep the bitterness from her tone.

"No, but I've known him longer. Did you ask him to explain?"

"I delivered a fabulous exit speech and left him standing in the newsroom with a group of really angry employees."

"Oh, boy."

"He tried to call—"

"He tried to *call?*" Taylor looked at her in amazement. "On the phone? Like a person-to-person conversation?"

Molly waved absently in the direction of her answering machine. "He left messages."

"Are you serious? Sam *never* calls unless he has to. You're sure it was him?"

"Caller ID," Molly supplied.

"What did he say?"

"I haven't listened to them."

Taylor surged from the chair and headed for the machine. "That was mistake number one, Molly. If Sam called you, then believe me, he definitely has something to say."

Molly groaned as Taylor punched the button to play back the messages. There were several from her friends, her parents and her sisters. Interspersed were Sam's three calls. The first asked her to call him back. The second *demanded* that she call him back. And the third all but threatened dire consequences if she didn't return his call.

Taylor gestured at Molly. "Mark my words, Molly, Sam wants you in his life."

"It won't work," Molly insisted.

"I'd say the real question is, do you *want* it to work?"

Molly didn't have to think very hard about that. Her heart already knew the answer. She was in love with Sam Reed. She'd been in love with him since the moment he'd shown her his sailboat and told her the story of rescuing it from near-ruin. Molly had always been a rescuer. In Sam, she'd found a kindred spirit. "Wishing doesn't make it so."

Taylor folded her arms. "Sam told me once that you were the gutsiest woman he'd ever met. Wishing may not get you what you want, but hard work and courage will."

"Taylor—"

"Are you willing to fight for him?"

"Don't you mean fight *with* him?"

"If that's what it takes. Is he worth it?"

"Of course," Molly said without hesitation.

Taylor's expression was simultaneously satisfied and calculating. "Then that's all I need to know."

## Chapter Eleven

Sam leaned one elbow on the bar in the ballroom of the Ritz-Carlton the following night and spoke to Taylor's hired bartender. "What have you got that'll fix a migraine?" Against his better judgment, he'd let his sister-in-law talk him into attending this damned event. They were half an hour into the thing and there was still no sign of Taylor. Sam had accepted all the good wishes he could tolerate.

The young man behind the bar gave him a shrewd look. "Headache or heartache?"

Irritated, Sam plunked his glass down. "Give me a soda water. Lots of ice and lots of lime."

"No booze?"

"Can't stand the stuff," he muttered. Tonight, he almost wished he was a drinking man.

"Sam?"

Sam stiffened when he felt the hand on his shoulder. He turned to find Mark Slenton, the governor's press secretary. "Mark," he acknowledged. At least this part of the evening might go well. He'd hoped to see Slenton tonight.

Mark shook his hand. "Happy birthday."

"Not so far," Sam muttered.

Mark looked at him curiously, but didn't press him for details. "I hope everything worked out okay on Thursday with that meeting." Mark had called Sam before his meeting with the reps from DOT and the governor's anti-fraud commission to ensure that Sam fully understood the governor's position.

"They were right on time," Sam assured him. They'd been friends since college, so Sam had reluctantly agreed when Mark asked him to consider what the two had to say.

"I hope they didn't cause you too much trouble. They were profoundly pleased that you agreed to hold the story."

Sam swirled his soda water. "I didn't agree to anything."

The other man's eyes widened. "But—"

"I told them I'd consider holding the piece if they could give me a compelling reason."

"Teasdale told me—"

"Then he misunderstood." Sam's fingers tightened on the glass. "First of all, I don't undercut my writers. Second, it might surprise you to learn that I don't especially like being asked to do the governor's political spinning. That's your job."

"Now hold on one minute, Sam."

"Third, I have yet to hear any reason at all why I shouldn't run the story, as planned, in tomorrow's edition."

"Damn it—"

"Besides the fact that this is an election year and the governor wants to prove he's actually accomplished something, frankly I don't think there is a compelling reason.''

Mark's face reddened. ''I told you we're working a state-wide crackdown. These things take time. We'd have gotten to Cobell eventually.''

''And thanks to a damned good reporter, you got to him before Massachusetts taxpayers had to bail out a billion-dollar mess. Hell, the governor ought to be giving Molly Flynn an award.''

Mark's expression was grim. ''Teasdale assured me you were going to work with us.''

''Then Teasdale should have stuck around for the outcome.'' Sam's head was pounding. The longer he considered what had happened in his office on Wednesday, the angrier he became. Worse yet, the longer he thought about it, the more he realized Molly was right. If he'd been making the decision for the *Boston Globe* or any other major market paper, he wouldn't even have considered Slenton's offer. Without realizing it, Sam had fallen straight into the stereotype Molly had created for him.

His gut tensed at the thought. Suddenly there was a blinding flash too near his face. Sam instinctively shielded his eyes. ''What the—''

A news photographer he recognized from his brother's wedding beamed at him. ''Just getting a picture of the birthday boy, Mr. Reed.'' The photographer glanced at Slenton. ''So, uh, are the Reeds exploring the political waters now?''

Sam had the feeling that if he was forced to spend another ten minutes at this monstrous event, his temper would spiral out of control. He gave the photographer a chilling look. "Hell, no," he said. "And before you ask, yes, you can—"

A commotion near the door caught his attention. Finally, he thought, maybe Taylor had arrived. As soon as he could, he was going to grill her about what she'd been doing with Molly for the past two days—and why Molly had yet to return his phone calls.

Sam saw Taylor's ostrich-plumed headpiece above the crowd. Without a word to Slenton or the photographer, he plunked his drink on the bar and shouldered past them.

The room suddenly came alive. Taylor's entrances had a way of doing that. He was halfway through the crowd when he began to hear bits and pieces of speculation. Taylor had someone with her—someone the crowd didn't know. God, he thought, let it be Molly. Sam craned his neck to see, but Taylor's damned ostrich plumes blocked his view.

"Sam." Amy stepped into his path. "Sam, wait." She laid a hand on his chest.

"Taylor's here," he said. "I want to know what the two of you have been hiding from me for the past two days. What have you done with Molly?"

Amy's smile was gentle and sweet. Sam had always liked that about her. She patted his chest as she took a moment to straighten the white rose in his lapel. "Just remember," she said, "the sweetest surprises sometimes turn up when you least expect them."

Sam didn't try to decipher the cryptic comment. He forged ahead. The crowd around his sister parted as he approached. He received several strange glances and was vaguely aware of the whispers around him, but didn't stop until the last person obstructing his view stepped aside. Then he realized what was causing all the speculation.

He stopped so abruptly that a waiter carrying a champagne-laden tray nearly collided with him.

Sam stood, heart pounding, mouth dry, and palms damp. He was looking straight into the clover-green eyes of Molly Flynn.

"Sam," Taylor said, her voice triumphant. "Happy birthday." She glided forward and wound her arm through his. "I'm sorry we're a little late, but girls need time, you know."

The crowd around them laughed. He thought. His ears had begun to ring. "What's the matter, Sam?" Taylor pressed. "You're acting like you've never seen a gorgeous woman before."

Not one like that. Molly Flynn, who had always had the power to knock the breath out of him, now stood six feet away in a crowded ballroom looking spectacular. Someone must have cued the band. They began a chorus of "Happy Birthday." People began to sing. Sam stood rooted to the spot, staring at Molly. Taylor gave him a none-too-subtle nudge. "I laid all the groundwork for you," she told him. "Now, go fix it or I might never speak to you again."

Molly, wearing a green velvet dress that hugged her curves and dipped and draped in all the right places, was fidgeting. The fidgeting gave him hope. Sam took a steadying breath and closed the distance between them. "Hi." Was that his voice? "Dance?"

She held his gaze for several seconds while he wondered why he couldn't think of anything else to say. Finally she moved an imperceptible step forward.

Sam placed a hand at the small of her back and drew her toward the dance floor. Her hair was piled atop her head in a cascade of curls and tendrils. She was taller than usual. A quick glance at her feet revealed two-inch heels, which made her slim ankles look slimmer and her long legs look longer. Sam's heart rate kicked up a notch.

When they reached the dance floor, he took Molly into his arms. The feel of her against his chest, one hand resting lightly on his shoulder, was so solidly right, he found it hard to believe that only two days had passed since he'd last seen her. He'd aged a decade, it seemed.

Sam tugged her closer as relief flooded him. She was in his arms again. Everything would be okay. For a man who never gambled, he was about to take the biggest gamble of his life. And for the first time since Taylor had told him her plans for this event, he was beginning to think the evening might actually turn out okay.

MOLLY SHIVERED against Sam's solid warmth. She'd spent the most miserable and anxious two days of her life waiting for this moment.

Sam lowered his head to hers. "You look spectacular," he told her.

"The dress itches."

A devilish smile played at the corner of his mouth. "What would you do if I told you I could take care of that? I have a suite at this hotel for tonight."

Her heart leapt. Maybe, just maybe, she told herself, Taylor was right. "Sam—about what happened—"

Sam shook his head. "Don't, Molly. You were right to be angry. I was ready to make the deal."

"Oh."

"You hoped you were wrong."

"No." Molly searched his face. "I just don't—I mean, I'm not sure now what—"

"Don't say anything else. Let me explain. You were right about a lot of things. You were right when you said I'd allowed the governor's office to trade on the Reed family name." His eyes darkened. "Hell, as far as I know, it might not even be my name."

"Your mother—"

"I told her yesterday to do what she wanted, that I wasn't paying her not to talk to the press."

"I'm sorry, Sam."

"Me, too," he said bitterly. "I told her if she needed money, I'd help her, but I'd never cared if Edward Reed was my father or not. I sure as hell wasn't going to start now."

"I think you did the best thing."

"And as far as the story's concerned, I haven't promised them yet that I'll delay it until Monday. Do you believe that?"

"I do," she assured him.

"However," he went on, "I did think I could persuade you to see it my way. You said I didn't take the *Sentinel* seriously, and in a way, I realize now that you were right. It doesn't mean as much to me as it does to you. I didn't see the harm in waiting a few more days to run the piece."

Molly thought that over. It was as she'd suspected. Despite Sam's protests, he'd never seen the *Sentinel* as more than a passing amusement, a favor for an old friend. He had no concept of what it meant to put down roots and build a life around something other people might find insignificant. Sam was like that stray cat she'd tried to befriend years ago. When he no longer needed her, he had chosen to move on. Molly felt the wound in her heart tear open again as she looked into Sam's eyes. "Then I guess the question is," she said softly, her voice slightly hoarse, "what *is* important to you, Sam?"

"*You* are, Molly. *You're* important. Don't you know that? I've been through hell the last two days."

She shook her head. "I don't mean what's important to you right now. I mean, ten years from now, twenty years from now. What are you going to look back on and say it mattered to you?"

"Molly—"

"Because if it's not people, then I feel really sorry for you. At the end of the day, family's all you've got, Sam. No matter how you come by them, or where you get them, they're all you've got. And you've spent so long trying to make sure you'd never get thrown out of one, you forgot you have to build it first."

The song ended and Molly took a step away from him. "I came tonight because I wanted to apologize to you. I realized I'd done exactly what you were always accusing me of—I had rushed into a situation and reacted with my heart instead of my head. But you know what, Sam? I'd rather be a person who does that and makes a lot of stupid mistakes than a person who never lets herself feel anything." Her throat felt tight. "That's a rotten way to live."

"Molly—"

She laid her hand on his chest. "No. Enjoy your party. Enjoy yourself. A lot of people have worked hard to show you they love you. Don't take that away from them."

He grabbed her hand. "You can't leave."

"I have to. I've got a life to get back to." She looked around the ballroom. "I don't belong here, but you do. Which is really what it comes down to, isn't it?"

"We can work this out."

"Not until you answer that question about your priorities, we can't. I know what mine are, and they probably aren't what you think, either." She tucked a tendril of loose hair behind her ear as she rose on tiptoe to kiss his cheek. "Happy birthday." And then she fled the room.

SAM STOOD ALONE on the dance floor and watched Molly walk away. Every instinct told him to go after her. He'd made the mistake of letting her walk out of the *Sentinel* on Wednesday, and it had taken until tonight for her to come back to him. This time, he had the feeling he was on the verge of ruining the best thing that had ever happened to him.

A hand landed on his shoulder. He turned to find his brother. "She's incredible," Ben said. Sam nodded. Ben's gaze remained on Molly's retreating figure. "And she's good for you."

Sam nodded again. "Yeah."

"You're in love with her," Ben guessed.

"Hell, Ben, I don't know."

"Is your head pounding and your stomach in knots?"

"Yeah."

"It's love."

"Then what the hell am I supposed to do about it?"

Ben grinned at him. "Damn it, Sam, I can't believe you're asking me that question."

"*I've* never been in love before. You're the expert on the subject."

Ben cast a quick glance at his wife who was standing near the bar deep in conversation with Taylor. The two women looked distinctly unhappy. He turned to his brother again. "You've always been a fighter," he told Sam. "You mean to tell me you're not willing to fight for the most important thing in your life?"

Sam gave Ben a sharp look. "What?"

"The most important thing in your life," Ben repeated. "At the end of the day, the only thing that really matters is who you love and who loves you. Wouldn't you say?"

If Sam hadn't been so shell-shocked, he might have laughed out loud. Molly had made the same statement, and then left him wondering how in the world he was supposed to come up with an answer for her. Fool that he was, he hadn't realized it had been staring him in the face for weeks.

Sam reached into his pocket and pulled out his cell phone. He dialed Greg Jessen's number. The new editorial director of the *Payne Sentinel* answered on the second ring.

"Greg? It's Sam." Sam accepted Greg's birthday greeting with only minor annoyance. "Yeah, thanks. Listen, I need you to do two things for me."

"Sure, Sam. What's going on?"

"I need you to call Cindy Freesdon and tell her to do whatever she has to do to hack into Molly's computer and see what the status is on her transportation story."

"I think it was just about done when Molly, er, left on Wednesday."

"I'm counting on that," Sam told him. "Cindy will know where to find it. Look it over and see how close it is to ready. If you need to edit it, just prep it to be a two-parter. We'll run the second part later."

"Okay. What's the other thing?"

"I need you to stop the presses," Sam said. Ben raised his eyebrows. Sam gave a few final instructions to Greg Jessen, then hung up the phone. He slipped it back in his pocket. He passed his brother the key to the presidential suite. "Here," he told him. "Taylor got this for throwing the party here. She wanted me to stay there tonight."

"I think she figured you'd share it with Molly."

"I think so, too. You and Amy take it. I've got other plans."

"Plans that include Payne, Massachusetts?"

"Yes," Sam said. He checked his watch. "And I've got to get on the road. The copy for my front-page edition is now five hours past deadline."

Ben laughed. "Stop the presses? You've always wanted to say that, haven't you?"

Sam grinned—his first real smile in two days. "Yeah. It felt good."

Ben nodded. "All right, I'll cover for you with Taylor. Tell Molly I said hello."

Sam was already heading for the door when he heard Ben call out to him, "What are you going to give me for not telling Taylor to start planning your wedding?''

Sam didn't bother to respond.

MOLLY HEARD the familiar thump of the Saturday morning edition on her doorstep. Weary and emotionally exhausted from the night before, she'd collapsed on the sofa when she'd finally returned home from Boston. Seeing Sam had drained her, but she'd expected that. What she hadn't expected was the horrible anxiety she'd felt as the waiting kicked in. She'd thrown everything on the table last night. All she could do now was wait and see what Sam would decide.

Nervous energy had helped her make the drive home from Boston, but by the time she let herself in the front door, she'd been a bundle of nerves. She'd managed to strip out of the velvet dress Taylor had helped her find, and had savagely run a brush through the obscenely expensive hairdo Taylor's personal stylist had executed earlier that day. A good scrub of the washcloth took off her makeup, and when she finally slid on her heart-and-lips printed pajamas, Molly felt better. Saner. But somehow she couldn't face the prospect of sleeping in the bed she'd shared—however briefly—with Sam. So she'd settled onto the couch with Errol, where she'd fallen into a fitful sleep.

The thump of the paper had awakened her. Usually she hurried to the door, but today the thought held little appeal. Her story should have been on the front page. Instead, when the paper had gone to press yesterday afternoon, the front-page article was a filler piece about the upcoming statewide elections. Molly contemplated going back to sleep, but Errol was nudging her hand insistently. He recognized the morning thump as the cue that Molly should be up and feeding him.

Groaning, she rolled to her feet and padded toward the front door. The sun seemed brighter than usual as she reached for the paper. Molly carried it back to the sofa and sank down wearily to scan the front page— more from habit than from interest.

Her eyes widened, and her heart kicked into double time when she saw the headline—her headline—announcing the discrepancies she'd uncovered in the mayor's election reports and giving information about the fraudulent bid process Cobell had used for the transportation hub.

Molly scanned the front page, noting that very little of her piece had been changed. Greg Jessen had done an outstanding job of editing it, she noted, as she thumbed through the front section for the continuation. A full-page ad on the second page of the front section stopped her cold. Laid out like a personal ad, it read:

WANTED: self-assured, confident woman to mend ways of arrogant, confirmed bachelor. Sam Reed, Operating Partner and CFO of Reed Enterprises, seeks a candidate of marriageable age who is looking for a serious commitment. The ideal woman must be able to tolerate Mr. Reed's unusually hard head and stubborn nature. She must be able to argue with Mr. Reed until he sees reason, have the tenacity not to relent when

he turns churlish, and the grace to recognize that
he will continue to make mistakes. She will need
the patience of a saint, the endurance of a long-
distance runner, and the heart of a warrior to put
up with Mr. Reed's irascible nature and often
unmanageable moods. Mr. Reed has a propensity
for redheads with green eyes and sharp minds.
The interested and qualified party who wishes to
apply should do so by opening her front door
where Mr. Reed anxiously awaits her.

Molly's hands trembled. She read through the ad
again, and then a third time to make sure she'd read
it correctly. Slowly, she stood and walked to the door.
She took a deep breath and pulled it open to find Sam,
looking tired, worn, and absolutely wonderful, standing on her front porch.

"Sam. How did you—"

He made a sweeping motion with his arm. "I
tipped your paperboy to let me deliver your paper.
You'll be happy to know I still have the touch."

Despite her fatigue, a smile played at the corner of
Molly's mouth. "I heard it hit the front door. Nice
thump."

"Yeah. Thanks."

In the morning light, he looked more relaxed than
he had the night before. She had the vague feeling
that she, on the other hand, probably looked as if
she'd been hit by a freight train.

Molly held the newspaper up. "I saw the article. I
was, um, surprised."

Sam shrugged. "I was wrong, and I'm big enough
to admit it. You deserved to break that story, and the

*Sentinel* deserved to be the paper that broke it. I lost sight of that.'' He scrubbed a hand over his face. "And while I'm at it, I might as well tell you I realize I've been wrong about other things, too.''

Molly felt her stomach flutter. "You have?"

He nodded. "Yes. You were right about me. I lost sight of what mattered. When I was a kid, I spent a lot of time worrying that I had nowhere to belong. I was angry at Edward Reed because I needed him and I didn't want to. And I was angry at my mother because she didn't need me.''

"Sam—"

He shook his head, a slight smile tugging at his mouth. "This time, let me finish, Molly.'' He took a step toward her, pulled the paper from her hands and tossed it aside. Cradling both her hands in his, he pulled them to his chest. "I have to admit that when you challenged me last night, I didn't think I knew how to answer you. I wasn't really sure I could tell you what mattered to me. To be perfectly honest, I hadn't given it a lot of thought. The only things that mattered to me were being independent and self-sufficient.''

Molly realized, now, the significance of what Taylor had told her about Sam's relationship with the Reeds. She understood why he'd never accepted Edward Reed's money—why he'd never been able to stand the idea of being reliant on his father. "I know," she said softly.

Sam continued. "And in doing that, I lost the most important part of myself.'' He rubbed his thumb over the back of her hands. He looked nervous, and a little on edge. "You saw the ad?" he asked.

Molly nodded. "That's a great deal on airfare to the West Coast."

Sam blinked. "Airfare? Molly—"

She laughed and let him off the hook. "Oh, you mean the full-page ad on the second page of the front section? Yeah, I caught that."

"I meant it," he said. "It's a lifetime commitment."

"Did you also mean the part about putting up with your moods and your hard head?"

"The whole package."

"I'm sure you'll get a lot of applicants."

"There's only one woman in the world who's qualified." He looked at her seriously. "It's got to be you, Molly. I finally realized it last night."

Her heart was racing, and her eyes felt suspiciously damp. "It was the dress, wasn't it?" she managed to quip.

He grinned at her. "Despite the fact that you looked drop-dead gorgeous in that dress—no, it wasn't the dress. Or the hair."

"Thank God for that," she said, "because I don't think I can live through another four-hour session with Phillipe. The hair thing is not going to be happening again."

Sam was smiling at her, with a breathtaking smile of absolute perfection that made her toes curl. "And as much as it turned me on to see you in that dress, I have developed an affinity for university sweatshirts." He folded her hands closer to his chest, and his expression grew serious. "No, Molly, it wasn't the way you looked. It was you—who you are. I let you walk out of the ballroom because I didn't realize that. Then Ben said something that put everything into focus. You'd said it before, but I wasn't listening. At the end of the day, family's all you've got.'' His gaze turned intense as he searched Molly's face. "I love you, Molly. I love you more than I thought I was capable of loving anyone. I want you to be my family."

With a slight laugh, Molly tumbled forward and fell into his arms. "Oh, Sam."

He held her close. "I'm screwing this up. That wasn't what I meant to—"

She threw her head back and covered his mouth with her fingertips. "It was perfect, Sam," she told him. "Don't change a thing."

"But I didn't—"

She shook her head. Stretching up on tiptoe, she gave him a quick kiss. "And yes, I'll marry you."

# Epilogue

*Two months later*

"Pass me the candle," Molly told her niece, Kelly.

Sam, Molly, and the entire Flynn clan, stood in the backyard of her parents' home in Payne. Despite the chilly December air, Sam felt warm. He watched Kelly reach solemnly for the lit candle. Her father helped her lift it from its holder and pass it to Molly. The flame flickered, illuminating Molly's face in a warm glow.

She was gorgeous, Sam thought, in so many ways. There were times when just looking at Molly made his chest hurt. Her spirit was beautiful. Molly must have sensed his scrutiny. She glanced at him and gave him a gentle smile that stole his breath.

She held the candle up and looked around the circle of her large family. "Okay, Sam," she said. "This is it. You ready?"

She had no idea how ready he was. In two months, she'd be his wife. Molly and Taylor had set the wedding for Valentine's Day. Molly had pointed out that while Sam might not know the actual date of his birthday, no one could take away the date of their anniversary.

"I'm ready," he told her.

"Okay, Kelly." Molly looked at her niece. "Go ahead."

Kelly stepped into the center of the circle and reached for Sam's hand. "Flynns," the child said seriously, "keep promises."

Katie joined her cousin and added her hand to Sam's and Kelly's. "Flynns," she said, "look out for one another."

Megan was next. She grinned at Sam as she joined the small group in the inner circle. "Flynns never cheat."

One at a time, the rest of the children approached Sam and added their statements to the growing list. Flynns don't lie. Flynns say they're sorry. Flynns admit mistakes. Flynns are kind. Flynns accept others. Flynns stick together.

When the children were finished they went back to their places. Molly handed the candle to her sister and joined Sam in the center of the circle. She wrapped her arms around his neck and smiled at him, a broad smile full of promise and hope. "All you have to do is say yes, Sam, and you belong to the Flynns."

Sam held her close, his heart almost impossibly full. "Yes, Molly. Absolutely yes."

With a light laugh, she went on tiptoe to kiss him. Her lips felt cold in the frosty evening air, but warmed quickly as the hot spark of passion that always lay just beneath the surface flared to life and stole his breath.

Sam could have stood there for hours in the light

of the full moon, basking in the warmth of this family that had taken him in so readily. He felt like the most blessed man alive. In two months, Molly would be his wife. They'd decided to live in Payne, where Molly would continue to work for the *Sentinel,* and Sam could commute a couple of times a week to Boston. He would still work with Ben, although the brothers had agreed to find a way for Sam to do less traveling.

The future looked better than it ever had to him, and Sam continued to marvel at his remarkable fortune.

Something cold and wet hit his arm with a thud. A spray of snow splattered against his cheek. Sam ended the kiss and raised his head. "What the—"

Molly started laughing.

"Aunt Molly," Kelly said. "Cut it out. Flynns don't kiss!"

Colleen urged her daughter toward the house. "Come on, honey," she said, giving Molly a dry look. "Let's go make some hot chocolate."

"But—"

"Now," Colleen said. "Let's leave Molly and Sam alone for a little while."

"But why?"

"Because there are parts of the Flynn initiation ceremony that are for adults only. I'll tell you when you're older."

When they were alone, Molly looked up at Sam. "It's a little corny, I know—"

He shook his head. "It's perfect," he said solemnly. "It couldn't have been more perfect."

She studied him in the moonlight. "You belong, Sam. I hope you know that."

Sam nodded. "You showed me. I love you, Molly."

"Oh, good," she said, her lips turning into a slight smile. "Because I love you, too."

Sam grinned at her for a moment, then, in a deft move, toppled her onto a snowbank. Molly was still laughing when Sam came down on top of her. He kissed her deeply, brushing her hair away from her face. "Thanks for having me," he told her. "Not just anybody would, you know."

"I have it on good authority that you're considered very eligible."

"Not anymore. I've found a qualified applicant for the position of Mrs. Reed."

"She must have the patience of a saint."

"And the body of a goddess," he said.

Molly laughed. "I think you need to have your eyes checked," she told Sam.

He shook his head. "She's perfect. I handpicked her."

A mysterious, womanly smile lit her eyes. "That's where you're wrong," she told him. "She handpicked you. Never forget that."

"Don't worry," he whispered. "I could never forget that. Not ever."

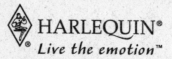

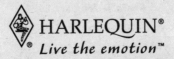

National Bestselling Author

# brenda novak

# COLD FEET

Despite the cloud of suspicion that followed her father to his grave, Madison Lieberman maintained his innocence...*until* crime writer Caleb Trovato forces her to confront the past once again.

**"Readers will quickly be drawn into this well-written, multi-faceted story that is an engrossing, compelling read."**
**—*Library Journal***

*Available February 2004.*

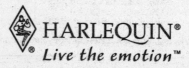

**HARLEQUIN®**
*Live the emotion*™

**Visit us at www.eHarlequin.com**

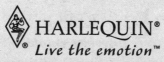

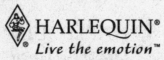